"Come now, *Princesa*. You had the nerve to propose marriage to me. Don't shy away now."

"I...I do not ask for your fidelity or your love, Gabriel. I...do not need such delusions in my life. I only ask that you give me..." Such color filled her cheeks that Gabriel stared transfixed. Her lips trembled and she dug her teeth into the lower one.

Lust punched him like an invisible blow, and it was all he could do not to tug that lower lip and taste her himself. "Eleni," he prompted in a harsh voice set on edge by the delectable temptation she made.

"I want a baby. A child of my own. I...was in the process of going through adoption agencies when you...you threatened to pull your company out of Drakon. It's not something I'm willing to give up on, for anyone."

Every muscle in his body stiffened. Every instinct he possessed warned him to walk away from this deal with this woman. "A baby? You're bargaining for a baby?" But even as he processed it, he had to admire her guts.

The Drakon Royals

Royalty never looked this scandalous!

To the outside world, the Drakon Royals have
the world at their feet. Yet beneath the surface,
black-hearted Crown Prince Andreas, his
daredevil younger brother Prince Nikandros
and their illegitimate sister Princess Eleni hide
the secrets of their family name...

Until one brush with desire, and each Drakon finds
themselves at the heart of their very own scandal!

Crowned for the Drakon Legacy

April 2017

The Drakon Baby Bargain

June 2017

Look out for Andreas's story

September 2017

*You won't want to miss this outrageously
scandalous new trilogy from Tara Pammi!*

Tara Pammi

THE DRAKON BABY BARGAIN

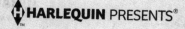

Recycling programs
for this product may
not exist in your area.

ISBN: 978-0-373-21348-1

The Drakon Baby Bargain

First North American Publication 2017

Copyright © 2017 by Tara Pammi

www.Harlequin.com

Printed in U.S.A.

Tara Pammi can't remember a moment when she wasn't lost in a book—especially a romance, which was much more exciting than a mathematics textbook at school. Years later, Tara's wild imagination and love for the written word revealed what she really wanted to do. Now she pairs alpha males who think they know everything with strong women who knock that theory *and* them off their feet!

Books by Tara Pammi

Harlequin Presents

The Sheikh's Pregnant Prisoner
The Man to Be Reckoned With
A Deal with Demakis

The Drakon Royals

Crowned for the Drakon Legacy

Brides for Billionaires

Married for the Sheikh's Duty

The Legendary Conti Brothers

The Surprise Conti Child
The Unwanted Conti Bride

Greek Tycoons Tamed

Claimed for His Duty
Bought for Her Innocence

Society Weddings

The Sicilian's Surprise Wife

A Dynasty of Sand and Scandal

The Last Prince of Dahaar
The True King of Dahaar

Visit the Author Profile page at Harlequin.com for more titles.

CHAPTER ONE

ONE KISS…

Eleni Drakos stood at the outer fringes of the black-and-white-tiled ballroom and peered through her elaborate mask.

One kiss from any man who'd look at her with warmth and desire, a man who could make her forget that a chasm of cutting loneliness was all that stretched ahead in her life.

One kiss because it was her thirtieth birthday and she was quite sick of her stagnant life, of pretending that the sight of her sister-in-law with her swollen belly didn't send a shaft of ache through her, or that she didn't crave a family of her own.

She'd lived her entire life within the rules her father, King Theos, had set, ensuring that her brothers, Andreas and Nikandros, had everything they had ever needed.

What she hadn't foreseen was that in the end, she would be alone. Just as she had been all these years.

She walked aimlessly at the fringes of the vast oval-shaped ballroom, the cut-crystal chandeliers making the resplendently dressed men and women glitter. She wasn't the only one hiding her identity behind the mask. The masquerade ball was an annual tradition of the House of Drakos and yet, with her father Theos's dementia becoming worse, it had not been held in four years.

But because the conservative traditionalists were balking at Andreas's continued absence after their father's death, and they feared that Nikandros and Gabriel Marquez's partnership was a risk to Drakon's economy, Eleni had suggested that they hold the ball again as a way of pacifying them.

And then she'd put the ball together in three weeks.

Scanning the stunningly dressed women and tuxedoed men who were dancing to a slow waltz, satisfaction filled her veins. Her fingers tingled to look through her fabled to-do list and check it off.

The black-and-white mask she'd bought on her trip to Paris last week went particularly well with the dark red lipstick. Piled high in a chignon, wispy tendrils of her usually unruly hair kissed her jaw.

Strapless and snug around her chest, her black-and-red silk ball gown accentuated an hourglass figure no amount of careful dieting could reduce, dipping at her waist and flaring into a full flounce.

The four-inch stilettos she had pushed her feet into boosted her five-two height, flashing her toned leg through the thigh-high slit. She'd been stunned when she'd looked at her reflection in the gold-filigree full-length mirror.

She'd always be plain compared to her half brothers, the Princes of Drakon; the media frequently reminded her by calling her the Plain Princess, but in that moment, she'd thought she had almost looked beautiful.

Good enough for the House of Drakos, her father would have said.

She continued wandering across the ballroom, marveling at the magnificence of the hotel.

It had been a crumbling Victorian-style mansion with out-of-date plumbing and bad interiors, but in three months Marquez Holdings Inc. had renovated it into a world-class destination for the nouveau rich that were pouring into Drakon, thanks to Gabriel Marquez's interest.

The ruthless real estate mogul was a guest of the palace of Drakon, and had been in Drakon for three months to oversee his company's investment in Drakon.

Casinos, luxury resorts that rivaled the King's Palace in style and ambience, mountain escapes, a world-class racing circuit—the map of Drakon was changing under Mr. Marquez's and her brother Nik's deft guidance.

A modern-day Midas, as the media called him, Eleni wouldn't have believed the transformation of the building Gabriel Marquez had wrought if she hadn't visited it herself almost a year ago.

Taking a sip of her chilled champagne, she looked down over the lush gardens. The scent of roses was thick in the air; a clock struck midnight at the old church in the city's main square.

She took a longer sip than was wise, felt the bubbly kiss her throat cold and sighed. It was a sound that seemed to come from the depths of her lonely soul.

The night stretched empty in front of her again.

"Why the long sigh, *querida*?"

The deep, slumberous voice sent a shiver down Eleni's spine that rivaled the tingles in her throat. Heart beating faster, she turned, bracing her hand on the balcony balustrade. "I didn't mean to interrupt your—"

"Stay."

With the one command, he made her spine lock. Even her father, who had been a bossy, hard-to-please man, had never ordered her around like that. "Excuse me?"

"Stay and keep me company," the man repeated, not even a little taken aback by her stiff tone.

With his back to the wall, the man was huge. Like a bouncer at a nightclub, he was tall and powerfully built.

A veneer of power clung to his frame. Unlike

the other men at the ball, no mask covered his face. Only shadows.

His blue-black hair framed his face in thick, unruly waves. The fine white dress shirt, unbuttoned at the throat, clung to lean muscle. The breadth of his frame sent tremors through Eleni.

She couldn't stop her gaze from traveling down his length. One foot crossed over the other and stretched the fabric of his trousers, revealing the hard musculature of his thighs.

Eleni swallowed the strange anticipation that seemed to rise in her throat. He pushed off from the wall.

She barely swallowed the soft gasp that rose to her lips.

Roughly chiseled masculine planes, a wide, sensuously cruel mouth and a nose bent in the middle—it was Gabriel Marquez, the very man she'd been mooning over for months. The man who reminded her she was a woman every minute she spent in his company. The desire and need that she'd thought had disappeared with Spiros still burned bright in her.

The ruthlessness that had made Gabriel a legend in boardrooms across Europe screamed from every inch of him.

Her heart pumped faster as she waited for him to recognize her.

His dark slate-gray eyes studied her. He'd never

so much as rested his gaze on her in three months of long meetings and numerous requests she'd dealt with. Not once had he shown any awareness that she was a woman.

No, then she was Princess Eleni Drakos, the facilitator for his firm, the grease between his company and the palace. But now she was a masked stranger, and something flared in those depths. Something that made her aware of how thin the silk of her dress was, of how tightly her skin seemed to be stretched.

"Such a wealth of regret and—" he paused while his gaze seared her "—need from a beautiful woman's lips...it feels like a challenge to any man."

"It wasn't...need," she retorted instantly, somehow negating what she had meant to say.

"Come, *querida*, isn't the idea of the masquerade to be open about our innermost desires while we hide our outward selves?" He traced the lower edge of her mask with a finger. Sensation zoomed from the spot. "You're safe behind that mask."

When his finger continued its journey back down and reached the indent over her upper lip, Eleni grabbed his wrist. If he touched her mouth... "Why aren't you wearing one?" she asked, wishing she didn't sound so breathless.

"Because I don't have to hide myself to express

what I want. Nor do I need to validate myself by hiding from the world who I am."

Arrogance dripped from his every word. But why not? There wasn't one single woman in the palace who hadn't lost her breath over the sight of him.

"You sound far too sure of your appeal."

He shrugged. "I am Gabriel Marquez, Ms....?"

Eleni racked her brains for a name that had no association with her or the House of Drakos. She'd taken every precaution not to betray her identity at this ball tonight, including arranging it so that she was thought to be still in Paris by her staff and even by her brother Nikandros. Only Mia knew she was here. And the last thing she wanted was for this man to figure out who she was, especially now that he was staring at her with such male interest that she felt heady and drunk.

"You didn't think of a fake name before you decided to come to the ball tonight?"

A taunt in his question brought her gaze to his. Humor lurked in his eyes and Eleni felt something in her loosen at the sight of it. The twitching curve of his bold mouth unraveled a hidden streak she didn't even know she had. "A name was not required for the goal I had in mind."

His gray gaze gleamed with pure delight. "Now you make me more curious. Still, I would like a name to call you as I figure out what specific goals you had in mind for tonight. And how I can help you succeed in achieving them."

Awareness flooded every inch of her body and Eleni stood shaking in its wake. His bold eyes swept over her face, stilling for a second more on her mouth. His nostrils flared and a wave of heat seemed to emanate from him.

He was attracted to her, she realized with a sudden leap of her heart. The man who had never given her a second glance was attracted to her.

"Cinderella," Eleni whispered, after a moment's thought.

His eyes crinkled at the corners and warmth filled his eyes. It was such an unfamiliar, unusual expression on his usually serious face that Eleni stared hungrily. The man was gorgeous, but his smile made him breathtaking. "And is it the cruel stepsisters and stepmother that you're hoping to hide from tonight, Cinderella?"

A smile came to her easily. As easily as the giddy response. She felt like a teenager, bantering and flirting with the boy she'd been sneaking glances at for a few months. Wild and beautiful and wanted, as if she were any one of those women who were even now skillfully laughing and flirting with available men, women who knew the cues and their own worth, women who would spend the night in a lover's arms.

Women who hadn't been waiting their entire life for a man who'd promised the world. Women who had the guts to go after what they wanted instead of mourning a man who was long gone from her life.

She hadn't thought Gabriel Marquez would be the one who'd seek her out, but in her wildest dreams, wasn't this what she wanted? So why not take what she'd come for? Why not live for the moment?

Why not believe in the fantasy that she was beautiful and desirable and confident, and that the fire she saw in his eyes was all for her?

"You were right on the first guess," she said, jumping into the moment with both feet.

A vertical line formed between his brows, his arms coming to the balcony to cage her. "You sound familiar, Cinderella."

Shoulders rigid with tension, Eleni fought to keep her face straight. Was it the way she had said his name? Or was her disguise not enough to hide who she was?

The levity disappeared from his eyes, leaving them stone cold. "Did you come to the ball looking for me, Cinderella?"

That set her back up like nothing else could have. Lifting her chin, she met his gaze square. "You think a lot of yourself, do you not?"

"Women seek favors of me all the time," he

said, the taunt back in his tone. "One does become a little jaded."

"It must be nice to believe the world revolves around oneself."

He threw his head back and laughed, sending trails of pleasure whispering over every inch of her skin. The broad shoulders shook with his laughter, which was a deep, masculine sound. Sleek grooves appeared in his rugged face, rendering that hard face a little beautiful.

"The more I listen to you, the more I like you. Tell me truly, have we met before?"

"In passing maybe," she offered, skating the line between truth and lies. "But I'm too much beneath your notice even if you'd seen me."

"I doubt I would forget you." The cage of his hands shrank around her, teasing her nostrils with the scent of him. Sandalwood and musk and something so essentially masculine it made her want to throw caution to the winds and burrow into his skin. "So if it's not a beastly family, who are you hiding from tonight, Ella?"

She flinched at the way he shortened her name and wished fervently that the shadows had hid it from him. Her brother Nik had always called her Ellie and so did Mia. To hear it fall from Gabriel's lips—it was thrilling and dangerous like nothing else.

"A clingy, dumbstruck lover?" Something hard entered his eyes. "Or a disgruntled husband?"

"No, no husband—" she half choked on the word "—and no lover either.

"I'm hiding from myself," she said, giving voice to the sentiment that had been gnawing at her for a while. "For one night, I wanted to be someone else, something else. I wanted to be daring and beautiful and a woman who lived in the moment. I wanted to be anyone but me." She caught the wistfulness in her voice and colored. "I'm sure you could not understand even if you tried."

He smiled and the grooves in his cheeks made his square jaw even more masculine. Straight white teeth gleamed in the silvery light, the lower lip jutting out in its fullness.

Having grown up surrounded by arrogant, unbending men like her father, King Theos, and half brother Andreas should have made her impervious to the aura of power that surrounded Gabriel, should have made her wary of that ruthless quality that pretty much had ruled her life when her father had been alive.

But it didn't.

For some unknown reason, she had always found herself drawn to Gabriel. To his confidence and arrogance.

"What makes you say that?" he ventured softly, as if he really wanted her opinion of him.

"You are Gabriel Marquez. Your reach and power…you own every space you enter, isn't that what they say?"

He shrugged, as if it were all matter of fact. "I have strived all my life to become what I am, to own everything I do today. And, no, I have never wished to wear another's skin."

Gray eyes searched her face. The perusal sent heat rushing to her cheeks. Long fingers drifted lazily onto her hips and every nerve in her body pulsed and stretched taut. As if it were possible to become smaller or less curvy by willing one's body to shrink.

If he noticed her instinctive reaction to his touch, he didn't heed it. Back and forth, his fingers traced the curve of her full hips, like butterfly kisses.

But it was rapt attention that went to her head, as if she had drunk something to make her euphoric. No man had ever looked at Eleni without the consequences of what and who she was.

Either she was an asset or a liability.

Either she was too low because she was illegitimate and held no real position of power in Drakos, or she was too much of a hassle to get involved with because she was close with her powerful brothers, the Princes of Drakon.

She belonged neither with the palace staff, nor on the wall of the East Hall that was graced by centuries of members of the distinguished, blue-blooded House of Drakos.

"Then my disguise, and my attempt at grabbing this moment under it, must seem like a joke to you. Pathetic even."

"You're wrong, *querida*. Even I need escape sometimes. Even I have to face the fact that I cannot control everything. That I cannot control fate and all the games it plays with us."

A thread of something in his tone tugged at her. As if there was something this powerful man needed that she could provide.

"I came...because tonight I cannot escape what tomorrow brings for me. Because tomorrow I face something I dread."

"Gabriel Marquez, afraid of something?"

Those grooves of his winked at her as he smiled again. "Shh...*querida*. You will spill my secrets and ruin my reputation. Now, tell me, what is it that you want tonight?"

The answer to a question had never come so easily before. "A kiss. I want a kiss." She swallowed at the flames of desire that licked at his gray eyes. "From a man who wants me. Not a pity kiss, Gabriel."

Hands on her hips, he swiveled her with masculine ease. Too shocked by the sudden contact, Eleni turned willingly.

A glass pane stood in front of them, reflecting their image. Even though she was wearing four-inch heels, he still easily overpowered her in height. She barely came to his shoulder. And his breadth—he was so overpoweringly male.

She felt like a doll, a fragile doll, compared to him. Not at all a practical, matter-of-fact woman, but a flimsy, fantastic creature of the night.

Even in the moonlight, it was clear that she was turned on. Her eyes glowed with gold flecks; her mouth, painted vivid red, was wide and vulnerable. She looked stunning, a mix of innocence and desire.

"Do you still think I would kiss you out of pity, *querida*?"

"No," she said loudly, the whisper of his touch filling her with a sense of feminine power.

Swiveling in his arms, she vined her arms around his neck.

When his cool lips slid over hers, Eleni jerked at the contact. For a huge man known for his arrogance, Gabriel kissed with a tenderness she couldn't believe. He tasted of whiskey and dark passion, and Eleni pressed into him shamelessly.

As if on cue, his kiss deepened. She gasped and his tongue flicked into her mouth. Stroked over the warm crevices with wicked intent. Tangled with her tongue in an erotic play that had her moaning.

Hard. Hungry. Hot. He kissed her like he wanted

to sink into her. Like she offered him that escape he desperately craved.

His kiss rained sensation upon her, set every nerve on fire. Eleni sank into him gratefully while his hands moved over her hips, up to her shoulders, and then clasped her cheeks.

Long thumbs traced the lines of her face, desire painted on his stunning features. He dipped his head again and took her in another stinging kiss.

Her senses in a haze, she barely paid attention to his words. How could she when he nipped at her lower lip as if he meant to devour her?

When he kissed her as though he needed her more than air?

Low and rough, his words sent shivers through her spine.

Cool air hit her eyes and only then did Eleni realize that her mask had loosened.

The warm, male embrace immediately turned into a cold frost. Heat dissipated from her and she had to blink to see.

Her delicate mask dangled from his fingers, and a scowl etched his brow. He stared at the mask in his hands and then at her. Again and again, back and forth, as if he couldn't believe the sight in front of his eyes.

Her lips burned with his kiss, but this was not the same man. He looked at her as if——she searched his expression—as if she had somehow betrayed him.

"What is the meaning of this, Ms. Drakos?" The mask fell at her feet with a whisper. "What the hell kind of a joke is this?"

She stepped back, the steel in his tone cutting through any foolish delusions she might still be clinging to. "It's not a joke. It's nothing," she whispered and turned away.

Barely had she gone two steps before a vise-like grip had clamped over her upper arm and turned her. "Why are you here tonight? What do you want from me?"

The nerve of the man! "*You* approached *me*. You…you ordered me to stay and keep you company. You…I only spoke the truth."

"So I'm supposed to believe the Plain Princess of Drakon—" he bit out her moniker with such sarcasm that Eleni flinched "—walks around masquerade balls, accosting men for kisses? That this is your nightly routine?"

"I did not accost you at all. And yes… I wanted a kiss. I wanted to feel less lonely for one night. I wanted…" Her voice caught, but she didn't back down. "Which scenario threatens your masculine ego—that a woman could want to kiss a man, or that in your arrogance you think I came here looking to somehow trap you into kissing me?"

"You lied to me, *Princesa*. I asked you straight

and you said you didn't know me. Maybe you even got a little power trip from the fact that you knew who I was and I didn't know who you were. Maybe it's a little game you play every night with powerful men."

"You're crossing the line!"

"I'm sick of deceit and lies. If it is a kiss you want, here it is!"

If Eleni had had any sense, she would have slapped his arrogant jaw, hard. But no, when he touched his lips to hers again, she melted. She had no will or control over her body.

When he licked the seam of her lips, she gasped open for him, like a sunflower.

When he plunged his tongue into the cavern of her mouth, she shamelessly pressed against him.

His hands moved to her bottom and he pressed her against him, until she felt the evidence of his arousal. Until the hard planes of his body were stamped onto her soft curves. Until she was moaning, spreading her legs to feel more of him.

The kiss was over before it had begun, and yet it seemed to spin her senses. And the man who had delivered it looked at her as if she had agreed to sell her soul for pennies. "If you're that desperate for a man, maybe ask one of your powerful brothers to set you up with one, *Princesa*," he said mockingly. "The next man you play your little game with might not be as forgiving as me for your duplicity."

Eleni stared at him, shaking from head to toe, burning with the unspent desire that he had aroused in her. Desire, she now realized, he had aroused with the sole intention of punishing her.

"I would not kiss you again if you were the last man on earth, Mr. Marquez," she shouted but he'd already gone.

Try as she might to fight the temptation, she couldn't help but run her fingers over her stinging mouth. Couldn't stop tasting him on her lips.

CHAPTER TWO

Three months later

"I HATE THIS PLACE, I hate that I had to give up all my friends and move here and I hate you."

The loud, blistering announcement exploded inside the conference room like a small detonation, jerking twelve heads toward the twelve-year-old girl standing just inside the room. Face scrunched, eyes brimming with fat tears, his daughter, Angelina, stood glaring at Gabriel Marquez.

A pounding began behind his left eye.

He had made his father's small construction company into a billionaire real estate firm, he owned major chunks of multinational companies, he had palatial residences in nine different cities in the world, but this was one problem, it seemed, for which he had no solution.

Angelina had come to live with him three months ago after her mother had passed away suddenly—a model he had met in New York, years ago.

His own daughter was a stranger, because until the accident that had killed her, Monique hadn't had the decency to tell Gabriel that he had a daughter.

Now Angelina looked at him as if he were a monster, as if he had taken away the one person who had loved her.

He hadn't been able to have one normal conversation with her in all the weeks she had been in Drakon with him.

"Angelina, calm down and wait for my meeting to finish," he gritted out. His jaw hurt with how tightly he had leashed the urge to vent his frustration that he was floundering just as much as she was.

That they were strangers to each other was not his fault.

His board members stared between him and Angie like spectators at a tennis match, ready to feed fuel to the wildly spreading rumors that Gabriel Marquez was an abysmal father.

Anything he did and said was news to the press. But the fact that he'd successfully hidden the existence of a daughter, who'd been born out of wedlock, for twelve years, sent them into a feeding frenzy. That his daughter hated him with every breath and, even worse, didn't know him at all would be the cherry on a very nasty cake.

"If I waited for you to finish one of your unending meetings, I would wait forever. All I want is to—"

Gabriel shot up from his seat, frustration boiling over in his blood. "You behave like a spoiled brat, with no concern for others' time. Has your mother taught you no manners?"

Her flinch fell on him like a poisoned dart, sinking deep. Goddamn it, nothing he said ever worked with Angelina. The tears that she had somehow contained in those big eyes fell onto her round cheeks, drawing paths down to her neck. "I wish you had died instead of Mom. I wish you weren't my father. I wish—"

"Angelina! That's enough," a feminine voice shot out.

Shock traveled through Gabriel as his daughter, who'd barely exchanged one civil word with him in three months, instantly looked contrite. Her round shoulders straightened and something shifted in the planes of her juvenile face, already struggling to show signs of adulthood.

He startled when Eleni Drakos pushed her chair back and walked toward his daughter, her expression one of sternness and yet somehow kindness at the same time.

Gabriel frowned as her pumps click-clacked against the marble floor. In three months, he hadn't been able to quite put his finger on the woman the media disparagingly called the Plain Princess.

An opinion he didn't agree with anymore.

Unlike her tall, dark brothers, the Princes of Drakon, Eleni Drakos, on first impression, was a mousy woman. Ten years ago, she'd barely ever met his gaze, hiding behind King Theos's fierce temper.

Since he'd arrived in Drakon a few months ago, however, he'd watched the brisk efficiency with which she ordered the palace staff around—and even his staff.

Every time he turned around, there she was, a petite dynamo. Only now, as he saw her reach Angelina, did he realize how much his staff and he had depended on her to smooth out numerous problems between his company and the palace in those first few weeks.

How much the Crown Prince Andreas and the Daredevil Nikandros relied on her.

His frown deepened as her slim hand went around Angelina.

She whispered something and instantly his daughter's expression cleared. A hesitation emerged in her eyes but Angelina wiped her tears, and then to Gabriel's shock, a tentative smile curved her mouth.

A tight ache emerged in the nether regions of Gabriel's heart. Three months with a string of nannies each more expensive and efficient than the next, three months of gifts and presents to make up for twelve birthdays, three months of fighting the urge to tell her that it was not his fault, not once had Angelina looked at him with anything remotely bordering on the affection in her eyes as she looked at Eleni Drakos now.

What magic had the Princess wrought on his child? To what purpose? When had Angelina become acquainted with her?

Shock buffeted him in fresh waves when Eleni softly nudged Angelina toward him.

The wariness in his daughter's eyes dealt a swift kick to his gut more painful and wretched than anything Gabriel had faced before. But for the life of him, he hadn't been able to forge even a tenuous connection between them.

It was as if fate was laughing at him.

He'd willfully become this man who avoided emotional entanglement at any cost. Now, try as he might, it seemed he couldn't connect with his own daughter.

"I'm sorry," Angelina whispered, her eyes bright and big.

She didn't call him Papa but he knew better than to expect a miracle. She turned to the Princess as if waiting for another cue, as if she could only bear to do this small thing—look at him without hatred—for the Princess.

Breath balled up in his throat, for he'd never felt this strange anticipation.

Hands firmly on those small shoulders, the Princess gave his daughter a cue.

Again, something about her smile snagged

him while she and Angelina walked toward him. That his daughter, who treated him as if he were plague-ridden, had found someone to connect with should have been a good thing.

Instead, all he felt was a yawning chasm in the pit of his stomach.

"Now, Angelina," the Princess said, and her voice shivered over his spine. The taste of her came to his lips, his hands fisting against the sensation of her curved hips. It was a sensation he hadn't been able to get out of his head in three months, even as he'd become more and more aware of her husky, low-pitched voice, of the way her dress shirts seemed voluptuous on her body, of the tug of her mouth on one side when she was being sarcastic, of her every movement. Of the fact that she'd avoided meeting his eyes since that night at the masquerade ball.

No woman had ever messed with his head quite so much by trying to ignore him.

I just wanted a kiss, Gabriel.

Had she?

And now here she was with a wide smile bestowed on his daughter.

Muddy brown eyes glinted with warmth, the edges of them tilting up, revealing hints of heritage no one, he was sure, knew about.

The smile seemed to spread to her entire body as she looked at Angelina. It snagged his attention, and every other man's attention, he noted with a flare of annoyance.

"Remember what we talked about," she said. "First we express our anger and hurt in a constructive way instead of hurling accusations at someone, however well deserved they may be."

His daughter nodded like an angel, lifting her chin in a show of condescension toward him. That put-upon anger and the skinny shoulders pretending to be so unaffected, caused Gabriel to feel a realization slam into him: hateful words or not, his daughter was very much just a kid.

And he wouldn't have seen it if not for the woman silently glaring at him over Angie's furiously nodding head. Her judgment of him was clear in her deepening frown.

"You went on your trip again. You not only left me with that…horrible nanny, but you also forgot my birthday. Mom would've never…" A choked sound emerged from Angie's throat. "Mom told me you didn't live with us because you were a busy man. Not because you didn't care about me. But now…I know she was lying to protect me. It's clear that you never wanted a daughter."

Pushing away the Princess's hand from her shoulder, Angie ran out of the boardroom, leaving a minefield of silence behind.

No, he'd never wanted a daughter. He hadn't

been in a relationship with her mother, which he thought was why she'd never told him.

And yet when he'd seen Angelina for the first time, Gabriel had known his life had forever changed. To his own surprise, he hadn't felt an ounce of resentment.

He'd only wanted to welcome her into his life.

But Angelina wouldn't give him a chance. Frustration and fury twisted inside him.

He took a few steps in her direction when he heard the soft command.

"Leave her alone, Mr. Marquez." A pregnant pause, as if the Princess couldn't believe her own audacity. "For now. Please. Don't force her to take back those words just because your ego is smarting."

A burning feeling emerged in his throat and Gabriel realized it was shame.

The Princess was right. He was only thinking about how this affected him, how he wanted to fight the tug of failure.

He'd moved mountains and built castles, immersed himself in the world's real estate games, and yet he didn't possess a single thing that would bring his daughter closer to him.

With one nod, he dismissed the meeting. He watched the quick shuffling of papers on the dark mahogany desk, heard the whisper of chairs as if it were all a background score, his attention fixed on the woman he had forced himself to ignore for three months.

And utterly failed.

He didn't want to have anything to do with this woman who'd made it so easy to unburden himself. Who had, for the first time in his adult life, made him question his choices, his very lifestyle. Made him wonder about the depth of love his father had nurtured for his mother, before it had destroyed him.

She shouldn't have spoken to him like that. She shouldn't have confronted him. She definitely shouldn't have chastised him as if he were a negligent staff member.

Eleni sighed as her hands brushed against her soft leather bag.

Now he'd probably forbid Angelina from even seeing her. And while she'd miss Angelina with an ache, it would be so much worse for the little girl.

Only last week had Angelina started opening up to Eleni, since she'd come to see that Eleni had no hidden agenda that involved her father.

And now, because she couldn't keep her mouth shut, because she couldn't bear to be ignored by Gabriel again, Angelina would lose the only adult she'd come to trust.

The hair on her nape stood in prickles as the room emptied around her.

Vibrating with a tension she couldn't dispel, she straightened from the table. Gabriel Marquez stood at the corner of the room, a silent specter studying her with hair-raising intensity. "You're full of neat little tricks, *Princesa*."

Eleni stiffened. "I have nothing to say to you."

He made his way across the room with soft strides for such a big man. Like a jungle cat. "I would say it was the opposite, judging by the looks you sent my way. I would say you were raring to rip into me."

Eleni tilted her head back, struggling to keep her gaze away from the hard contours of his mouth. His lips had been so soft and demanding against hers. So full of passion and tender warmth. For days afterward, she'd marveled at the paradox of the man's kiss, which matched the man himself—one moment warm and inviting, and the next cold and ruthless.

"Even the board members now know that you were dying to set me down about Angelina."

Heat rushed into her cheeks and she struggled to keep her thoughts and her gaze from straying. "I…was trying to defuse the situation without further breaking her—" she flinched as his gaze became chilly "—heart. Even you must agree that Angelina's feelings are the most important in that scene."

"Even I?" His taunt was voiced in such a low

tone that Eleni had to tilt closer to understand. Instantly, she was suffused in his male scent. Tendrils of warmth settled low in her belly as he reached her. "Explain."

Any mortification she felt at her body's alarming reaction to his nearness died at his curt tone. "Don't bark commands at me."

His gray eyes were cold and bleak, like a winter sky. "Maybe you think I'm one of the staff you order around with such brisk efficiency, *Princesa*. It would be in your best interests to remember who I am."

She tried for a laugh, awareness flooding through her. His hands had traced her hips as if she were a precious treasure. His body had been a fortress of warmth. She couldn't stop that rush of sensation so she held herself rigid instead. "Like you let anyone forget. This is ridiculous, Mr. Marquez. If you want to say something, then say it."

He breathed out in a harsh exhale, tension wreathing his features. "Angelina and you have formed a bond."

"Is there a question in that?" she taunted, ignoring the rational voice that said she was pulling the tail of a tiger.

He hesitated and Eleni saw something in those cold eyes that made her hesitate, rethink her opinion of him. Or at least not to condemn him so easily. "How? When?"

"When what?"

"When did you become close? How did you... have so much access to her?" His frown deepened as he searched her face. "It's not like you sit around playing the charming socialite in the palace."

Was he complimenting her or setting her down? Infuriating man! "I...I... The task of setting up quarters and such for the string of nannies you employed for her fell to me. When you disappeared on your long and frequent business trips, the task of making sure they did their job fell to me. I think it was the second one. Or the third. The poor woman couldn't find Angelina one day for hours and raised an alarm.

"You were in... Sydney, I think. Since you brought her to Drakon," she couldn't resist adding, "I noticed that Angelina always drifts toward the stables. I found her there that afternoon, hiding in my mare's stall. Angelina loves horses— did you know that? I invited her to spend some time during the day with me at the stables. And we...we got close," she finished, her face a swath of color.

Somehow, spending time with Angelina had become the high point of her day. Had filled the gaping hole in her life after her father's death and Andreas's uncharacteristic departure.

"But what did you do? And why? I want to

know what you did to get so close to her, Ms. Drakos."

He looked so befuddled that Eleni bit back her temper and sighed. "I didn't do it for some nefarious purpose."

He ran his hands through his hair, tight grooves etching around his mouth. "I'm not accusing you," he said, though his tone did just that. "I'm curious as to what you did, what techniques you employed, what…incentives you offered to get close to Angelina."

"She's not a business deal you're trying to close," she burst out, remembering her own confusion at that age.

"I have never lost a business deal in my life."

"That's exactly what I'm saying." She exhaled roughly and willed herself to be patient. For that twelve-year-old, if not for the arrogant Spaniard in front of her.

For three months, she'd tried to pretend that the kiss hadn't happened. That it hadn't been the most glorious moment of her life, even when he'd pushed her away with such apparent disgust. That her heart didn't speed up every time she laid eyes on him.

That she didn't hope in the farthest corners of her heart that he would look at her with that passion in his eyes again, that he would see her as a woman and not as a part of the palace machinery. That he would kiss her again, just one more time.

But no.

Five layers of makeup, a dress that displayed every curve and a sign around her neck that said she was willing and wanton. And of course, her identity hidden behind a mask.

That was the only way he would want her apparently.

She swallowed away the disappointment as she always did, tired of her own pathetic longing. There were years of his company's work still to be done in Drakon. Was she going to spend the next decade mooning over one kiss that meant nothing to him, like she had mourned the last decade over Spiros and his vows of undying devotion, even after he'd disappeared like mist?

"Angelina, for all that she's been forced to grow up in the past few months, is a little girl. With feelings and emotions. She lost the one person who loved her unconditionally. She's been thrust into an unfamiliar world with a man—"

"It has been eight months since her mother died."

"Eight months is an entire lifetime for her. You can't just...buy her things and expect everything to be all right. You can't just slot into her life and expect her to love you like she did her mother. Not by leaving her with a string of nannies. Not by engaging her in a battle of wills. And definitely not by demanding her affection and love."

"Those nannies came highly recommended with years of experience in dealing with kids."

"But not a single one of them tried to understand her. It was all just schedules and milestones and you can't just ignore…" She swallowed the lump that rose in her throat.

He tucked a finger under her chin and tilted it up. "I can't just ignore what?"

She wished she could hide the expression in her eyes. Erase the hurt from that corner of her heart that never seemed to heal. "You can't fix the loss of her mom by throwing her into the deep end. She's among strangers in a foreign country and she barely sees you. She…she told me last week that she wanted to run away because of what that ghastly girlfriend of yours told her."

If he wasn't holding her chin in his hands, she would have missed his flinch. "She's not my girlfriend. She's an ex. She…said she had experience with kids…that she could help me connect with Angelina."

Now she understood the lineup of exes and "girlfriends" that had been appearing outside his office in the last few weeks. It had taken every ounce of her willpower not to march in there and demand that he send them away. For Angelina's sake.

"Could you not see that they were just using Angelina like some stepping stone toward you?"

She saw it sink in. His jaw tightened. "And you, *Princesa*? You do not have any purpose?"

His gaze promptly fell to her mouth, a languid stroke against her senses. "I told you—I have no designs on you."

"You knew who I was and yet you still kissed me."

"Because my requirements for that night were to kiss a man. You fit the bill. If you hadn't ripped my mask off, I'd have been on my way and no one—"

"If I hadn't ripped the mask off—" his harsh breath purred over her cheeks "—I would have been *inside you*, right on that balcony, with your brother and half the world watching."

Gravelly and low, his words rippled over her skin. Places she shouldn't be thinking of throbbed with need. "Ripping off the mask was the only sensible thing that happened that night."

"I would have—" she licked her lips as if that could stave off the heat pouring through her "—stopped you. It wouldn't have gone that far."

His gaze held hers, amusement and something else glittering there. "Either you're very naive about men or you just like to lie to yourself." A rough exhale left his mouth. "And now I find you, of all the people in my life, bonded with my daughter."

Eleni pushed away from him, needing respite from that overwhelming masculinity. Respite from her own reactions. "Even your conceit can't be that great to think I befriended Angelina with some…underhanded intentions. Sitting in the stables by herself, she reminded me of myself."

"A Princess of Drakon, daughter to King Theos and sister to powerful Andreas and Nikandros— and I'm to believe you understand how Angelina feels? That you have to hide beneath a mask to find a man to kiss you?"

She shrugged, the gleam of interest in his eyes making her heart thud faster. If not for Angelina, he wouldn't have spared her a single glance again, much less a conversation.

"I don't care what you believe about me. Angelina needs to feel like she's important to someone, like there's some constant in her life that won't desert her. She's a sweet girl underneath all that bluster."

"She's sweet with you," he bit out, a vein vibrating in his forehead. "The first time I saw my daughter was at her mother's funeral. It took her a week to understand that I was indeed her father and not some terrifying stranger who was ripping her away from everything familiar. I learned after my ex was in an accident that she had named me as Angelina's father.

"In three months, she hasn't stopped looking at me as if I...were the culprit.

"My own daughter looks at me as if I..." He swallowed hard and looked away. "I've tried to be gentle with her...I've tried gifts. I've tried everything under the sun but not a damn thing works."

Eleni hoped for the little girl's sake that he would learn to express that concern. To show that he cared. But she'd been around too many thickheaded men, and Gabriel Marquez had proved that night that he was the king of arrogant ruthlessness and wouldn't recognize tender emotion if it hit him in that all too gorgeous face.

He'd connected with her that night when he'd thought her a stranger. But as soon as he'd learned her identity, as soon as he'd learned that she knew him, he had shut down. Had closed himself off so fast that for days after she'd wondered if she'd imagined their exchange.

She wanted nothing to do with such a hard man, a man who thought showing his emotions was a weakness.

But for Angelina's sake, she wanted to help. She remembered all too well how alone and frightened she had been growing up in the palace. It was only when her father had married Camille, Nikandros's mother that Eleni had realized that not everyone in the palace resented the illegitimate child that the King had adopted in a fit of uncharacteristic generosity.

Camille had been so busy with Nik's frail health, and yet she'd always had a kind word for Eleni.

"Never let him see a weakness, ma chérie,*"* when Eleni had cowered in the face of her father's rages. *"Never let them make you dispensable,"* when Eleni had, in her innocent ignorance, complained that the Crown Prince Andreas, the older brother she loved so much, didn't care about her either.

So Eleni had taken Camille's advice to heart and made herself indispensable to her father and brothers. She had never imagined becoming the buffer between the three of them.

As she'd observed this father and daughter over the last three months, she'd assumed Gabriel was the same as her own father: controlling, bloated with arrogance, treating his offspring like pawns in his own personal game.

The glittering frustration in Gabriel's eyes gave her hope for Angelina.

"She feels that you've taken her on as a last resort. With me, she knows I love spending time with her. That I don't expect anything in return, that it is not a duty."

Gabriel's gaze moved over her, searching without seeing her. She'd seen that look on her older brother Andreas's face—when he saw people only as a means to an end. When he decided on a course and set upon it, no matter what the cost to others. Her heart thumped in her chest.

"Then you'll teach me how to get through to her," he added softly, utter resolve in his tone, "and you'll help the both of us connect."

"It's not something I can transfer from my head to yours."

"I do not care what you call it, *Princesa,* but you'll teach me how to connect with my daughter." Stubborn resolve made his features look harsher than ever. "And you will do it before it's too late."

"What you're suggesting is…not that simple."

"I will speak to Nikandros about releasing you from all your many unofficial duties. From now on, you'll spend your entire time with Angelina. And me, whenever I'm available." His brow cleared, everything falling into place in his world. Even her soft gasp didn't divert his attention. "I'll try to clear my schedule for a couple of evenings every week and we will dine together. After a month or so, the three of us can take a trip together. I want to find a good school for her and you can accompany us."

The man's nerve! "I'm not your servant to be ordered about. I will not drop everything in my life just for your benefit. I will not..." She couldn't even get the words out at his arrogance. "You insult me with one breath, and then order me around on the next."

Spending months in his company, wishing he would take notice of her, comparing herself to his parade of girlfriends—it would be her personal torture device. "What makes you think I would willingly sign up for anything that concerns you?"

"Because you do not have anything going on in your life. I've been watching you, *Princesa*."

Eleni jerked back, her heart thumping against her rib cage. "Watching me? For what purpose?"

He shrugged, just like she'd done before. And if Eleni hadn't spent an hour with him on a moonlit terrace sharing the depths of her soul, she wouldn't have seen the carefully manufactured gesture. She'd have missed that utterly male gleam in his gaze.

"To figure you out."

"And what have you figured out?"

"You're illegitimate, so you don't rank that high with the traditionalists of the country. You have no boyfriend or lover and no options on the horizon, unless you ask your brothers to set you up. And they are smart enough to keep you around because of course you're sensible and reliable.

"I've seen you with your brothers and the staff. You're a very maternal sort of woman. You know every staff member by name, and you ask after their families. You give hours of your time to children's charities instead of just throwing money at them. And your reckless actions that night prove how desperate you are for your life to change. For it to be more than it is."

Shock robbed Eleni of speech as she stared at him. He'd so efficiently reduced her life to a cold, hard summary, a truthful one. "First I was deceiving, now I'm reckless?"

"Imagine if it had been anyone but me. Imagine if it had been one of the media or a man who could have harmed you in some way. You don't walk around parties advertising you're available, not when you're the bloody Princess of Drakon."

Eleni stared stupefied, the unease in his eyes far too real for her to scoff at. "I...I wouldn't have just walked off with any man."

He raised that arrogant brow and she flushed and looked away.

They both knew she'd have done whatever he wanted of her that night. And that awareness stood between them, taunting her.

"Allowing that you truly care for Angelina, what I suggest would not be a hardship at all. All I ask you is that you spend your time in the lap of luxury with Angelina and me."

"For how long?" she whispered, unable to resist. Unable to walk away from him.

"Until such time as I feel you're not needed anymore."

"So you're offering me a job?"

"Call it whatever you want, Princess. Money, jewels, stocks…you can have whatever you want in return."

A job description with a tenure and conditions. Just another man demanding his due without giving anything back. Just another role for her to play for a limited time. Like she'd always done, filled with the nauseating hope that it would last.

The reliable, responsible daughter to her father.

The buffer between her brothers.

The woman that the man she'd loved had easily and thoroughly forgotten.

The illegitimate but adopted child of the House of Drakos.

All temporary. All meaningless, in the end.

If she accepted his "offer," she would lose a bit of her heart to that little girl, and when she'd served her purpose, Gabriel would calmly remove her from his life. And yet, she wanted to do it. She wanted to spend time with him and Angelina, wanted to help them bridge that gap before it came irreparable.

She wanted to see more of the man she'd talked to that night. Heart thudding dangerously, she admitted that she wanted a chance for him to notice that she was a woman, to remember that he'd kissed her with such abandon.

She jerked in place when he cupped her jaw and tilted her face up to meet his gaze. Slumbering heat glittered there, reminding her of what had happened the last time he'd touched her. Tempting her. Her hesitation was ammunition as he cornered her with a predatory gleam. "Admit it, Princess." Eleni shivered when his hot breath caressed the rim of her ear. "You're tempted."

"Whatever I learned about you that night, I...I kept it to myself. I...trusted that man. But you... you play dirty, Gabriel."

"I play to win, *Princesa*. I always have." His brow rose as he searched her gaze. "It is clear that you truly care for Angelina. And if you agree, maybe I can be persuaded to overlook your deception." His thumb traced the line of her jaw, a featherlight stroke that branded her. The sound of her harsh breaths filled the silence, her body swaying toward him with a will of its own. She raised her gaze, frowning.

"I could even be persuaded to kiss you again, *Princesa*. I could give you all the excitement you crave, all the daring moments you want. I might even be willing to show you the passion that you desperately want.'

Toes scrunched in her sensible pumps, body

thrumming like a tautly stretched string, Eleni stared into his beautiful gray eyes.

His breath caressed her lips, his gaze studying her as if she were the most beautiful woman on earth. She felt drugged, and he hadn't even touched her. "So you're offering me—" somehow she spoke "—an affair in return for looking after your child?"

"We want each other, yes? It's not a big leap from that."

What would happen when she spent days in his company with just a little girl for buffer? What would happen when he didn't stop the next time? When she'd be all twisted and tangled into their lives and he decided he didn't need her anymore?

Where would she land then?

In the same place, with her heart bruised again by another careless man.

Better that she and Angelina cut that cord now before the damage to that young girl was permanent. Before Eleni herself forgot that no man was worth the heartache that she'd already tasted, thanks to Spiros. Thanks to her father.

Love was not for her, whatever silly dreams she wove.

She put her hand on his wrist and pushed it away. Her palm burned at that innocent contact. Her body whimpered silently at the promise in his eyes. "No."

"No what?"

"No to everything you suggested."

"Why not?"

Suddenly, the idea she'd been playing with in her head for a while now was the only lifeline. She would go away. Away from this man and his little girl who already owned a part of Eleni's heart. Away from the unending void that her life had seemed to be lately. "I plan to leave Drakon for a while."

His jaw tightened. From one breath to the next, his gaze became hard, all the heat gone. "How long is a while?"

"Months. Maybe a year." She stepped away, needing the distance. "I've always wanted to see the world and this is my chance."

"And what about Drakon and your duties? What about your precious brothers?"

"Nikandros has convinced me that they'll be here for the rest of our lives. I've never once left Drakon. I've seen nothing of the world beyond this palace and its walls. It is time for me to step out."

Time for her to reach for what she wanted.

Spending all this time with Angelina, nurturing their relationship, seeing the joy that came into the young girl's eyes when she and Eleni spent time together—it gave form to what Eleni herself desperately craved.

She would never love a man. But being a mother to a baby, bringing love into a child's life—someone unwanted, like she'd been—*that* she could do. That was in her hands.

"I wish I could help you, at least for her sake. But I just can't. I can't put my life on hold for anyone. Not anymore."

"When do you plan to leave?"

"In a week maybe. At the most, two. I would like to break it to Angelina with you there. I… I don't care whether you believe me or not, Mr. Marquez, but I do care about her. *So much.* If you care about her, and it seems like you do, then tell her that. Show it with your actions.

"And please, stop letting your ego get in the way of it."

CHAPTER THREE

"Is it true?"

Gabriel sighed and turned toward the figure standing just outside of his suite. As if entering it might force her to concede that he was a presence in her life, his daughter stood at the threshold, staring at him as if he were the enemy.

Somehow, he made his tone even. "Angelina, come inside."

She instantly stiffened, her bony shoulders poking out of her T-shirt like spikes. "I don't want to come inside. I just want to know if it's true."

"What is?"

"Ms. Drakos, is she leaving Drakon?" Damn it, he'd hoped she hadn't heard it yet. "Did she tell you?"

"No," he lied, feeling a hateful powerlessness within. It seemed nothing he offered could induce the Princess to stay. "But I heard one of the staff talking. They said she's going away for a while."

"Will she come back soon?"

His jaw tight, Gabriel shrugged. "It's possible, yes. She...said she might be gone for a month or two. She has her own life, *pequeña*." The Princess had made that very clear. And looking back over their argument, Gabriel cursed. For a businessman who thrived on negotiations and sweet-talking opponents into his camp, he had acted like a fool. Pushed all the wrong buttons.

Just as she did in him.

The sound of a soft whimper from his daughter jerked his head up. Christ, he would welcome the rebellion over this dejection in her eyes.

"Angelina, you will see her again. And even if Ms. Drakos leaves, you will make new friends. And I'll always—"

Tears drew paths over her cheeks as his twelve-year-old leaned against the wall and sobbed silently. Something twisted in his chest and Gabriel fisted his hands.

He reached her and even in the midst of her tears, she shrank from him. He caught the curse that wanted to escape his mouth and waited.

Roughly, and with a self-sufficiency that smacked of someone much older, she wiped at her cheeks and looked up at him. Retreated into herself. "Everyone leaves me. First it was my granddad. Then Mom. Now Ms. Drakos."

"*I* won't, Angelina."

"That's what you say."

"What can I do, Angelina? Tell me."

"You could ask Ms. Drakos not to leave. If you truly care about me, Mr. Marquez," she drawled in her American accent, as if such a thing was an impossibility, "you will somehow make Ms. Drakos stay."

Even the request was made with such resignation, such lack of faith that Gabriel felt winded.

Before he could answer, his daughter turned and walked away, her shoulders dejected. Without once looking back.

"He wants you to be his daughter's nanny?" said her sister-in-law Mia, who was heavily pregnant with twins, on their morning walk around the gardens Nik had had built for Mia.

Eleni nodded. "Wants? More like ordered me. You should've seen him, Mia. He got this look in his eyes, like he wasn't seeing *me* anymore. Just a solution to his problem."

That would make everything right in his world, like all arrogant men expected from those around them.

In the week since Gabriel had made that outrageous offer, she hadn't heard from him. Hopefully, he'd come to his senses. Yet, Eleni continued to feel his considerable power like a shadow over her life.

The gardens were a riot of color, the sky a perfect blue. All in all, it had been one of those perfect Drakon autumn weeks. Everything was ripe and coming to fruition.

She'd made some inquiries into the orphanages

in Drakon and submitted her paperwork. It could take months to get through the bureaucratic red tape, but a fierce sense of rightness filled her. And in the meantime, she was planning her trip.

It might not be as long as she'd suggested to Gabriel but it seemed like the perfect thing before she had a child of her own and the responsibility that would go with being a single mother.

"You refused, yes?" Mia probed.

"Of course, I did," she replied, as her gaze shied away from Mia's unbearable concern. Mia knew Eleni was attracted to Gabriel Marquez, that Angelina was coming to mean more and more to her every day. She felt naked, as if all her desperate longing was written on her face for everyone to see.

I could even be persuaded to kiss you again.

Humiliating heat filled her cheeks. She should've slapped the arrogant man.

"I'm worried about you, Ellie." Mia clasped her fingers. "You're getting far too attached to that little girl. I saw how upset she was a few days ago…"

Swallowing the lump in her throat, Eleni tried to sound casual. Angelina's crumpled face wouldn't leave her alone though. She'd been wrong in thinking she could walk out of Angelina's life without hurting her. "I'll be fine, Mia. If anything, these last few months with Angie have shown me how much I would like a baby of my own."

Mia sent her a stunned glance just as they saw Nikandros walk toward them.

"What the hell is going on between you and Gabriel, Ellie?" Nik said, loudly enough for some of the garden staff to look up curiously.

Eleni frowned. "Just a disagreement about his daughter. Why?"

Nik looked away and back. "He's threatening to pull Marquez Holdings out of Drakon if you don't cooperate with his demand."

"Cooperate? He can't do that!" Eleni's heart sank to her toes. She'd known he was ruthless, but this was beyond belief. "Can he, Nik? I know Andreas had his reservations about Gabriel but I thought we had an ironclad contract."

Nik pushed his hand through his hair, visibly shaking. "We do. Legally, he can't just pull his company out of Drakon. But the last thing we need in this economy is to get into a legal battle with him. He could raise a hundred issues and stall all our projects. He's…everything Andreas said he is when things don't go his way—an utter bastard. He's already canceled two of the investor meetings for no good reason."

Eleni rubbed a hand over her forehead, frustration coiling inside her. Just when she'd finally decided what she wanted in life… "I'll do anything for you and Andreas and... Drakon, Nik." Her daredevil brother had never seemed so anxious. "I'm sorry for—"

"*Christos*, Ellie! I don't blame you for any of this."

Eleni swallowed the lump in her throat. Her brothers did love her. Curse the blasted man for making her doubt it.

"All he keeps saying is that he wants *full access* to you. When I said you were not a resource to be loaned out, he had the gall to say that Andreas and I use you." Nik looked away from her, shame filling his eyes.

"Nik, you can't let him get to you like that." And yet, Gabriel had pinpointed both her own fear and apparently Nik's misgivings like a laser pointer. He rooted out weaknesses and he didn't care what he did with them.

Fury coursed through her veins.

"He didn't say anything I haven't been thinking the last few months. What does he want with you?"

"He wants me to help him forge a connection between him and his daughter. Be...available to them. Make it a priority in my life. When I told him that I was planning to travel, he—" She shivered, remembering the look in his eyes. He hadn't said anything and yet Eleni had known the matter was far from over. "He's desperate and he's pushing back."

"Stop being so damned generous, Ellie."

"I don't like what he's doing any more than you. Given the state Angelina was in when I told her, I..." Tears filled her eyes, frustration coiling inside her. "I feel guilty. I didn't realize how attached she was getting to me. And now, if he walks away from Drakon, it will undo everything Andreas and you are trying to do. There's only one solution."

"I can't let you be his daughter's nanny, Ellie. Haven't you given enough to this family and Drakon?" With another curse, Nikandros pulled her into his arms and Eleni went like a rag doll. The familiar scent of her brother calmed the panic in her tummy.

She knew, just as Nik did, that the ruthless Spaniard had left her no way out. He knew she'd do anything for her brothers. And Angelina too.

Gabriel held all the cards but Eleni had the blood of stubborn warriors in her veins, however tainted her father had thought it.

She didn't intend to let the arrogant Spaniard take anything that she didn't want to give.

She had come to him finally, bristling with righteous fury.

And dressed to kill.

Gabriel watched, transfixed, as Eleni Drakos waited by the steps, awareness jolting him.

The white stone of the restaurant showed off that innate elegance, that quiet grace of hers, reminding him that legitimate or not, she was very much from the illustrious House of Drakos.

The setting sun caught the copper highlights in her shoulder-length hair. Her face didn't have those arresting, stark angles her brothers' did. Nor symmetric features, with her too-proud nose that was clearly inherited from her father. She was neither conventionally beautiful nor had the haughty elegance of a woman born to one of the most distinguished royal houses of the world.

And yet there was a fresh, voluptuous beauty to her form.

The pink fabric of her dress barely kissed her knees and skimmed her lush curves like a lover's hands every time the breeze pressed it against her body. A white metal ring circled her neck, from which the dress flowed down. It bared her rounded shoulders, exposing miles of golden skin.

Up close, the dress was an invitation to sin. A birthmark on her fragile collarbone, the rounded curve of her hip, those long fingers of hers that she used to tuck a stray lock behind her ear—everything about her hit Gabriel like a blow to his solar plexus.

Why had no man stolen her away from under her brothers' control?

What had he been thinking, taunting her with the promise of desire between them?

"You're staring, Mr. Marquez."

Something floral floated toward him. "I've never seen you in a dress, *Princesa*. You look—" he leisurely swept his gaze over her, and saw a rewarding blush steal up through her cheeks "—stunning."

"And of course you're surprised by that," she said dismissively. If he weren't obsessed with every small detail about her, he would have missed the quiver in her voice. The quick flick of her lashes to hide the widening of her eyes.

Was she truly so unused to a man's attentions? Had no man ever wanted her? Touched her? The last thought consumed him. He frowned. "Surprised? What do you mean?"

"You thought I would come here with my tail tucked between my legs, desperate for your promise. Desperate for your—"

The picture she painted made him smile. "If you keep saying it, I promise, *Princesa*. I will begin to like it."

"Like what?"

"You being desperate for me. In any and every way."

She gasped, her eyes voluptuously wide in

her lush face before she flicked those thick lashes down.

The lower lip jutted out in a silky pout. Painted a soft pink, her mouth was a lush invitation. "I needed to feel good about myself today, Mr. Marquez. Sort of like being equipped for war."

"This is war for you?"

"Are you saying it isn't? I don't bend to your will like every other being on the planet so you threaten what I hold most dear. The last thing I need is to be riddled by my own insecurities in the midst of it. I have no intention of letting the press coin another—"

"I do not agree with the—"

"You'll find that I'm the most sensible, practical woman you've ever met and yet you have the…alarming ability to make me lose my faculties."

He stared at her slack-jawed for a few beats before he burst out laughing.

Shoulders rigid, hands fisted, she stood with a patient look.

"Here I assumed you'd dressed up for the simple reason of impressing me. That you were hoping to make *me* lose my faculties."

The tight purse of her lips said it had crossed her mind. "How I dress reflects on my brothers and the House of Drakos, so really, this—" she did a sweeping movement with her hand over her dress, and Gabriel smiled "—has nothing to do with you, Mr. Marquez. You have made the little squabble between us into a national matter. I... could give it no less importance."

Gabriel felt a sting of irritation at the mention of her brothers. He held her elbow and nudged her toward the entrance of the restaurant.

"My daughter's happiness is not a little squabble."

"It isn't." She sighed, her shoulders dropping. "Which is the only reason I'm here to negotiate. Nikandros would rather you sink everything than let me come here, let me bargain with my life. But I can't allow you to go on some macho rampage on Drakon just because you aren't getting your way. Neither can I bear to ignore the fact that I miscalculated."

"Miscalculated what?"

Such raw emotion flickered in her big eyes that Gabriel took a step back. Used to sophisticated, modern women, who, like him, thought emotions were weaknesses, who played games with his head and body, the Princess was a whiplash against his senses.

"How my departure might affect Angelina. I didn't realize how attached she has grown to me, how she could see this also as abandonment." Her mouth trembled, her eyes wide in her face. "The sounds of her tears won't leave me alone."

Gears turned in his head as he evaluated the situation.

There had to be something she wanted that he could provide. Everyone, especially women, wanted something from him. Even his friend Alyssa, who was full of integrity, had needed his backing when she'd first started out.

He was convinced that she would be the best thing for Angelina—she had proved it to him a hundred times over the past two weeks, even as he'd threatened everything she held dear.

A soft gasp from her lush mouth was her only sign that she'd noticed the empty restaurant. They followed the concierge to an intimately laid out dinner on the famed terrace that offered panoramic views of mountains that bracketed Drakon on one side.

The crystal flutes and the champagne bucket glittered in the orange light of the setting sun. He watched the open expressions on her face—awe, a flicker of joy when she saw the mountain peaks followed by dismay and then that practical, nothing-will-efface-me sensibility of hers.

Interesting was an understatement when it came to her.

He held the chair for her. Her usual grace fluttered when she almost slipped. Hand at her elbow, Gabriel straightened her. The slide of her lush curves against him startled an instant reaction from his body. "Thank you," she murmured in a throaty whisper that brought images of her lush limbs beneath him.

Bathed in the setting sun's light, she made a stunning figure. Anyone who saw her now would never call her plain.

Gritting his jaw, he willed his body to calm, his mind to focus on the moment. This was the most important meeting in his life and he didn't intend to fail tonight.

"Champagne?" he asked after they settled down.

The pulse at her throat flickered madly, yet when she raised her gaze to him, it was quite steady. "I'm so stupid," she scoffed, her mouth twisting into a bitter curve.

He frowned, not liking the shutters that fell over her eyes, hiding her from him. He hadn't realized how much of a lure Eleni Drakos's artless honesty was until she shut it away. "I don't know what you mean."

She raised her arms and moved them over the empty restaurant, the gorgeous view of the sunset, the bucket of champagne. "Even after all your threats and insults, I didn't regret…seeing you that night. I held on to the belief that until you ripped off my mask, it had been a genuine moment between us. But you just can't help yourself, can you?"

"Princesa—"

"You will use everything I told you, everything I feel when I see you…to the last drop, to manipulate me to your will."

Something in the curve of her mouth made Gabriel bristle. Guilt was not an emotion he had ever liked nor had any use for. "I do not see why it is such a hardship for you to spend some time with me and Angelina. Not when you claim to truly love her."

"Because my life is not a stopgap measure for you."

"Yet it is for your father, your brothers and even Drakon, is it not? What do I have to do to buy that same loyalty toward Angelina? What is it that I have to do to ensure that you stay in Angelina's life for as long as she needs you, for as long as she and I need to make a connection?"

Her heart fluttered like the wings of a trapped bird. Her fingers shook around the stem and Eleni hid them in her lap. "You might regret making that offer."

"There is no condition of yours that I would *not* meet, *Princesa*. The world will be at your feet if you agree."

She licked her pink lips, and his body tightened. Gabriel swallowed a curse. Really, his attraction to her was becoming a problem. For he knew now that his desire to give her what she'd wanted that night hadn't come solely so that he could bend her to his will. It had come because he'd wanted to explore it with her. And still did. He wanted to taste that lush mouth, he wanted to run his hands and his mouth all over her curves, he wanted to possess her until all the prim propriety that she used as a mask was unraveled, until that self-sufficiency she wielded as a weapon against the world was undone.

Until she was the woman who had kissed him with such hunger that night.

"I want a signed agreement from you that you'll never again put Drakon's economy in jeopardy, ever."

He sat back and took stock of her. Mouth tight with resolve. Eyes glittering with temper. He smiled and took a sip of water just to make her wait for his answer. She fidgeted in her seat, glancing away from him. The woman was good.

"Done," he said finally. "As long as you meet with all my conditions."

"I'm not finished yet."

"Go on."

"I want that agreement as part of a prenuptial contract. I want Drakon and your company bound tightly so that you can't threaten us like this again."

He jerked his gaze from her lovely mouth to her eyes, shock flooding him. "What did you say?"

She pulled her tightly clasped hands out of her lap onto the table, then brought them down again. When she looked at him, resolve filled her features. "I've been over what you want of me a thousand times in my head. Of the number of ways you could hold the threat of Drakon over my head. Of how easily you...you would use what I told you about my life, about me that night for your own advantage. Of how fragile Angelina has been since she heard of my plans."

A soft gasp escaped her mouth, as if this pained her.

"The last thing I want is for her to hate you or blame you when she loses me. The last thing I need is for you to do this to Nikandros all over again because I didn't make her love you in four months. Or whatever ridiculous time frame you think this needs to happen in. I just can't take that chance.

"So I've found a solution that works for all parties and that will not permanently damage the innocent in all of this. I...I want you to marry me. You will use Drakon to ensure Angelina's well-being, and I'm hoping you would think twice about destroying it when it becomes as much her life as it is my own. I want...a chance to do right by myself too."

This time, when he laughed, it was full of sarcasm. Anger fueled him at her outrageous suggestion. "Let me enlighten you, Princess. You will not do right by yourself by hitching your cart to me. I'm incapable of developing romantic feelings for a woman. You'll only be—"

"It will not be a true marriage. I know what I'm bringing to this arrangement and I know what I'll be getting." Eleni would not tie herself to another relationship with yet another man and end up wondering what she lacked all over again. "You would be ensuring that Angelina has a mother who loves her."

"And you would do all this for your precious Drakon? Expect nothing else from me?" Even as he challenged her, her willingness to martyr herself bothered him. Did neither Nikandros nor Andreas care about her future? Was there no one to look after the damned female?

"No, I do want something…"

"Come now, *Princesa*. You had the nerve to propose marriage to me. Don't shy away now."

"I…I do not ask for your fidelity or your love, Gabriel. I…do not need such delusions in my life. I only ask that you give me…" Such color filled her cheeks that Gabriel stared transfixed. Her lips trembled and she dug her teeth into the lower one.

Lust punched him like an invisible blow, and it was all he could do not to tug that lower lip and taste her himself. "Eleni," he prompted in a harsh voice set on edge by the delectable temptation she made.

"I want a baby. A child of my own. I...was in the process of going through adoption agencies when you...you threatened to pull your company out of Drakon. It's not something I'm willing to give up on, for anyone."

Every muscle in his body stiffened. Every instinct he possessed warned him to walk away from this deal with this woman. "A baby? You're bargaining for a baby?" But even as he processed it, he had to admire her guts.

"Yes. As far as the outside world is concerned, as far as Angelina is concerned, we'll be a family. I'll help you forge a connection with her. I'll not make any demands of your time or your emotions. I'd love her as if she were my own. We will lead separate lives except when needed by our children."

"If only the media could see you now... Mad King Theos taught you politics well. Even your brothers I'm sure could not have come up with a better strategy to bind my company to Drakon."

She flinched and shrank back into her seat. She looked down into her lap as if to hide her stricken expression. "You think I *want* this? To marry a man who looks upon me as if I'm trapping him, a man whose affairs are notorious for their short shelf life, a man I have to negotiate with for a child? It will be a marriage of convenience, Gabriel. You will do it for Angelina and I for Drakon."

Any idea that the Princess was manipulating him dissolved at the fury in her eyes.

Gabriel pushed away from the table and went to the empty, glittering bar. Silence stretched in all the spaces between them as he examined his own emotions. That anger he wanted to hold on to was fleeing fast. No one could accuse the Princess of Drakon of being without logic.

He ran a hand through his hair roughly as he heard her movements. Felt the heat from her body stroke his senses. Once she was with him and Angelina, in whatever capacity, he knew that he would have the Princess of Drakon in his bed. The attraction between them was far too consuming.

But for the first time in his life, he could not do as he wanted. He could not take the Princess to his bed and spoil the chance of Angelina having her in her life.

Would an amicable arrangement between them, masquerading as a marriage for the world, for the sake of his own daughter, be so bad? Would binding the Princess to him in the most legal means be the best for his daughter?

"Being a father... It's a role I still haven't settled into, with Angelina. You want me to give you another child knowing that he or she will always look at me and feel as if I've rejected them."

Such ache resonated in those last words that Eleni felt her own heart twist at them. In a matter of seconds, he changed from an arrogant, ruthless businessman to a man familiar with pain. The man she'd met on a moonlit night.

She grabbed his hand with hers on impulse, forcing him to relax his fist. "But you will not be a failure. You will have me to guide you. I know what it feels like to be that child, Gabriel. I know what that kind of a father looks like. I would not expose a child of mine to such a father. You're not that man.

"Your desire to do the right thing by Angelina is what landed us in this…situation. As much as I hate that you hold the fate of everything I love in your hands, I understand your reasons. We will just be a couple who shares children and who loves them. Successful marriages are built on less."

"And if I say no?" He turned toward her, numerous overhead lights wreathing his hard features with a deceiving softness. "Will you walk away from Angelina? Will you let ruin come to Drakon?"

Eleni forced herself to give him a smile. Or as close to a smile as she could get. Negotiating with Gabriel was like banging glass against a rock.

Nik had warned her, outright forbidden her from doing this. But what choice did she have?

Loving that little girl, loving Drakon and her brothers had never felt like a boulder around her neck.

"Yes." Whether she'd be able to withstand it, she didn't know. But she couldn't let him ruin Drakon. Not when she could stop it. "Angelina will hate you for what you're doing. Drakon and its people will suffer. And it will all be on your own head."

Eleni didn't wait for his answer. She'd had enough of the seesawing of her own feelings. Enough of bargaining for the one thing she wanted in her life.

If he didn't agree to this, then he was truly a ruthless bastard, she repeated to herself. A man whose heart was so deeply buried that he might as well not have had one at all.

She'd reached the small courtyard outside the restaurant when she felt his hand on her shoulder. Heart thudding in her chest, she turned around. The black shirt and trousers he wore blended in with the darkness surrounding them, leaving only an outline of the sheer breadth of his shoulders, of his imposing height.

Of his overwhelming masculinity and what she'd boldly demanded of him.

Both his hands landed on her shoulders now

and tugged her toward him. As if he too was struggling to see her in the scant moonlight.

His fingers bit into her flesh. "An arrangement then, *Princesa*? No demands, no expectations?"

"Yes," she said, licking her lips. Longing twisted through her when her legs tangled with his. Her hands landed somewhere on his chest, where his heart boldly thudded underneath one palm. Hard muscle and slumbering heat—there was so much of him that Eleni felt suddenly fragile, feminine. "No demands and no expectations."

"No fidelity required?"

"Not after you give me a baby." She tried to sound matter-of-fact but goodness, he was too much man. Her voice sounded husky, uneven instead. "Really, Gabriel. It would not be a bad idea for you to curb your…activities in that area in the short term anyway. Let Angelina see you make her a priority. Not your business, not your love life. But her. Let her see that we love her, and we're in this together, for her. In the meantime, you could…we could…"

His white teeth gleamed, giving her a hint of his feral smile. The sound of his mocking laughter lashed against her senses. She felt utterly drowned in the scents and sounds and feel of him. "So I'm allowed to sleep with my wife until then but no longer?"

"Precisely." Embarrassment burned her and

Eleni suddenly thanked the cloak of the night. The devil gleamed in his smile, winked from the glitter of his eyes. Taunted her with the sound of his mockery. "I suspect that by that time whatever novelty I hold for you will have worn off. As long as you're discreet with your affairs, it will not affect the children or me."

He cupped her nape with such possessive intent that Eleni shivered. Rough fingers crawled up into her hair, tilting her head up. "You've got all the little details figured out, haven't you? Princess Eleni Drakos to the rescue, huh?"

She'd no idea whether he was still teasing her or if he was angry. All she could do was feel. Feel the imprint of his fingers on her scalp. Feel the hard contours of his hips against her belly. Feel the hot beat of his breath against her face.

"And you, *Princesa*?" Suddenly, his lips grazed hers, and she jerked at the streak of heat that raced through her. She whimpered when he did it again, never settling his mouth against hers. But teasing and taunting, delighting and declaring the fact that she could have him sign a hundred contracts and check a hundred conditions, but when it came to this fire between them, when it came to the slide of his lips over hers, she bent to his will. "Will you seek out lovers when you want a man in your bed in some later years too?"

She raised a drugged gaze to his, and fierce

masculine satisfaction filled Gabriel's every vein. Her finger pads pressed into his chest and he wanted to feel them all over him. He wanted her beneath him, all lush, glorious curves bare, the polite mask she wore unraveled. He wanted that woman from the masquerade ball in his bed. "What?"

The thought of a lover hadn't even entered his mind for months now. How could it, when he was obsessed with the little warrior in front of him? But the thought of her with another man... no, she would not need another man, he promised himself.

If the Princess wanted an amiable arrangement, he would give it to her. But only after he had spoiled her for any other man. "Will you look for a lover, Eleni? When this marriage becomes an arrangement again, when you do not need me?"

"I would never do anything that would harm my kids or damage the reputation of the House of Drakos."

"Right answer, *Princesa*," he whispered, before dipping his mouth to hers.

Shivers passed through her slender frame before she stiffened in his arms. Blood rushing south, he bit that lower lip that always tortured him and with a husky groan, she opened her mouth.

He dipped his tongue inside it, holding her head

for his onslaught. She tasted of heat and innocence, her tongue tentatively coming to tangle
with his.

If he had had any reservations about her counterproposal, Gabriel forgot them, lost in the hunger raging through his body.

The Princess in his bed, and a bridge between
his daughter and him—maybe this marriage
wasn't such a bad idea for the near future.

CHAPTER FOUR

PLAIN PRINCESS SNARES
REAL ESTATE TYCOON!
Love match or convenient arrangement fixed
by her powerful brothers?

ELENI TRIED TO ignore the bald headline she'd seen on a popular social media site that morning as she walked toward Gabriel's apartments in the palace's west wing.

At six foot three and with a muscular frame, he was sexuality incarnate. Add the reach of his name, the sheer confidence that seemed to exude from his very pores, his talent as one of the foremost architects of their time and his real estate empire—Gabriel was every woman's dream man.

Yet, he had remained an elusive bachelor for so many years that the world's gaze had shifted to the woman who had persuaded him into a momentous commitment. For the first time in her life, Eleni was the center of attention, and the limelight only made her uncomfortably aware of how poorly she measured up to him in the world's view.

When she and Gabriel had broken the news to his daughter, Angelina had thrown herself into

Eleni's arms, her lanky frame shaking from head to toe. That they were doing right by the little girl had stopped Eleni from questioning the sanity of it all as the media and the palace had been thrown into a whirlwind at the news.

The very morning after their deal had been agreed, Gabriel had invited Nikandros and her to a meeting. From the man who kissed her like his life depended on it to the ruthless businessman in the boardroom, the transformation in him was radical. Furious, Nik and his lawyers had pushed to fill every small loophole that Gabriel could use to back out again while he had sat there, calm as you please, dictating the terms of their marriage and sending curious looks her way.

Angelina was already skipping on the front steps, excited about spending the evening with Eleni and her father. Eleni went into the sitting room. Finding it empty, she went into his study.

High windows poured sunlight over the tall, broad form bent over his desk. Sleeves rolled up to his elbows showed corded forearms dusted liberally with dark hair. His pencil and scale looked like tiny implements in his huge hands and yet there was a kind of grace in his movements as he measured and drew on the tabbed white sheet.

Heart palpitating at dangerous speeds, Eleni noted the stretch of his black trousers over his buttocks and thighs, the tight stretch of his shirt over his back muscles.

Jet-black hair fell over his forehead and he pushed it away.

He was immersed in his work—a design for a new resort at the foot of the mountains in Drakon.

And yet, as she stared at the lean fluidity of his powerful body and caught the soft susurrations of the pencil across the paper in the background, all her insecurities came rushing forth.

Had she actually imagined that she would share a bed with him, invite him into her body, and then remain unscathed?

A hundred thoughts crowding her mind, she turned to flee, just as long fingers clamped over her arm.

The scrape of his fingers over her bare arm was a spark over the ignition. Sensation swirled beneath her skin. Every atom of her being wanted to savor that touch.

"Running away, Eleni?"

His soft taunt raised the small hairs over her neck. "I..." She licked her lips, her mouth utterly parched.

The impact of his touch hit her afresh, the imprint of his hard mouth on hers, the grip of his fingers over her hips... His dress shirt was unbuttoned to his waist, displaying tanned golden skin dotted with sparse black hair. The corded muscles of his throat, the afternoon stubble on his jaw... Eleni closed her eyes to process the devastation he caused to her very equilibrium.

He smelled of cologne and male sweat, an irresistible combination that seemed to fill her senses. Something in the lazy twitch of his mouth reminded her of a tabby cat far too sure of his appeal.

"I was just waiting to see if there would be a break in your focus." Somehow, she managed a steady voice. "My father lost his temper if I so much as bothered him in his office. Even when I had an appointment."

"You needed an appointment to see your father?"

"He was a busy man and, at that time, it wasn't like I was adding any value to the administration."

When he stared at her mutely, she shrugged. He had a way of looking at her that made her feel naked, and not in the physical way. As if she was still the girl who'd been told that the King was her father and that he'd done a great service by acknowledging her as his, let alone adopting her.

To push Gabriel's attention away from her, she said, "Angelina and I have been waiting. For over thirty minutes."

He frowned, and then looked at the big dial on his wrist. "Damn. I completely forgot." Fingers wrapped around the nape of his neck as he studied his work area. In months of working with him and his team, she had never seen him hesitate like this. Never seen him be anything but confident and arrogant, even forceful in his will.

"Is she mad at me?"

"No, she said I was foolish to be surprised that you hadn't shown up," she said, finding her balance again. Talking about Angelina—that she could do. "That much cynicism in one so young, it's not healthy."

"I...was working and forgot." He glanced back at his desk, pushed his hair away from his face. "Maybe it is better if I didn't join you this evening. We're both still reeling from our last disagreement."

Eleni sighed, remembering the staff telling her about the pastries they'd found in the toilet and the pumps that had been shredded to pieces as a result. A thousand-piece puzzle—a map of the United States—was spread out all over the palace. Eleni and Mia had found poor New York in the garden and had laughed nonstop at the girl's imaginative destruction.

The whole palace and its mother knew of the row that had resulted between father and daughter when he'd found out what she'd done.

It seemed Gabriel couldn't stop ordering more

and more expensive gifts and Angelina couldn't resist new and imaginative ways to destroy them.

"My daughter and I have matching tempers, *Princesa*. I have learned that it is wise to stay away from each other when we are riled. I might say something that would cause permanent damage. So, it's probably a good idea for you to continue on to whatever entertainment you've planned for tonight."

"For goodness' sake, Gabriel, can't you look beneath her rebellious actions?"

"She shredded the pumps. She threw the diamond earrings in the garbage. I…"

"Because she wanted *you* instead. Gabriel, she doesn't understand yet that you'll keep her. That you'll be permanent in her life. That you won't abandon her like her mother has done. She keeps rejecting anything you give her."

Eyes like the coldest frost pinned her. "I don't want a lecture, Eleni."

"I don't care what you want. It is my job—" she spanned her hands around them "—to tell you what you're doing wrong. Stop being so manly and bullheaded about it."

"Manly and bullheaded?"

"Yes, like all thickheaded men. Look past your own ego."

"You think me an awful father, *Princesa*, but since I learned of her existence, I have made changes to my life that I have never done for anyone before. I brought her here, I live with her, I've made concessions for her. What else do I need to do?"

"You need to spend time with her, Gabriel. Is that so hard to see?" When he continued to frown, Eleni sighed. "You say you want to bridge the gap between you. You say she is important to you. But in the two weeks that we have agreed on our...deal, you have either postponed, canceled or found an excuse to avoid spending any time with us. *With her.* Angelina sees through your actions and that's the message she gets."

"She seems overjoyed by the fact that you will not be leaving."

"She is."

"Then what else does she need?"

"Did you think I would replace you?" Suddenly, she felt a piece click inside her head. She stared at him. "Something in you resists the effort at forging any real connection with her. Is it any wonder she thinks you don't want her?"

Gabriel stared at the sudden softening of Eleni's eyes and looked away. His jaw gritted, his head hurt at the realization that the Princess was right again. He had done everything his research said he'd have to do, except spend time with his daughter.

He heard the Princess's soft tread, the scent of

something floral coiling sinuously around his sore limbs. After his row with Angelina, he'd been working nonstop, burying himself in tasks. Because here, there was no place for failure. Here, there was no place for vulnerability, especially his.

"Gabriel...all your intentions will be for nothing if your actions don't back them up. What is it that you find so hard about this? Please, let me understand."

"There's nothing I find hard, *Princesa*."

Instead of walking away, she put her hand on his arm, a soft tinkling laugh falling from her mouth. "How like a man to say that."

He turned around, intending to set her down. Yet when he looked at her, the soft light of her brown eyes stole through him, loosening up hard places inside him. Making him remember things he'd rather forget. "I had custody of my half sister, Isabella, when I was eighteen while my mother was cleaning up her own act."

"She was engaged to Andreas but she..."

He swallowed the frustration that sat like a lump in his throat. "Had an affair with Nikandros, yes. Isabella was just like my mother, flighty by nature, never settling on one thing. And I think the fact that I resented her only made it worse."

"You resented her?"

"I don't know. I think I did. My mother had her

after she deserted my father and got pregnant by her lover. When they came back, she was pregnant with her. My father died a couple of years later and Isabella became my responsibility, I was hardly the loving older brother. At that point, I barely…"

"What, Gabriel?"

"I barely trusted a woman. I…was busy building my empire.

"I always felt guilty that I might have pushed Isabella over the edge with my judgment when she was just an innocent. That, had I been a better brother, she would have had more security. Every time I see Angelina, I remember my treatment of my sister, I guess."

"And you think you'd rather not try than risk failing?"

"Isn't it better that she hates me, that she holds me responsible for everything that happened to her rather than me messing her up even more? What if she sees my resentment of her mother? Won't she be caught between her mother's memory and loyalty to me?" His gaze was far-off, his mouth rigid with tension. "Like you say, maybe I decided it was better this way."

"Then please let me tell you that it is not. Every time you cancel on her, every time you put work or something else before her, you're losing a little more of your daughter, Gabriel. Please, trust me to help you through this. Trust that I will not let you fail. Or else all of this is useless."

Gabriel lifted his gaze to Eleni's, something inside him shifting. He'd never trusted a woman with anything. Of course, he had friends that he liked, even respected, but trusting a woman... He'd lost that ability even before his mom had walked out on him and his father.

He'd lost it when he'd seen her break her promise again and again. He'd lost it when instead of being the adult, she'd filled his ears with her own struggles. He'd lost it when she'd forced him to grow up too fast.

Her brown eyes wide and open, Eleni looked back at him. The lift of her chin, the tilt of her mouth—she radiated a perplexing combination of confidence and innocence that fascinated Gabriel even now.

He glanced down at her fingers moving over his, felt the fragile pulse at her wrist beneath his fingers. In the week that they had announced to the world their plans, she'd come under close scrutiny by the media.

Every single one of those write-ups had been uncomplimentary toward the Princess, while he had been hailed as the perfect catch. Her background had come under scrutiny—the fact that her mother had been Andreas's nanny and had an affair with the King under the Queen's nose, that her mother had effectively sold Eleni to the King, that since no man had ever shown interest in the Plain Princess this match with Gabriel had been orchestrated by her powerful brothers.

Yet, the Princess had only held her head higher through all the dirt dished by the press, had only carried herself with the dignity that seemed to have been bred into her very bones, while he and Nikandros negotiated their prenup contract in which she gave generously of herself to Drakon.

She'd wanted no accolades, no acknowledgment for what she'd done.

The only time she had interrupted the negotiations had been to ask, with a flush staining her cheeks, that any children they might have would be provided for.

For all her alleged dirty blood, the Princess of Drakon was an asset to the House of Drakos. A woman unlike anyone he'd ever met.

A woman Gabriel didn't quite know what to do with now that she was going to be his. A woman who unnerved Gabriel in how generously she loved his daughter and her brothers.

He took her hand in his and turned it over. Traced his fingers over the dips and highs of her palm. Heard the soft flutter of her breath every time he touched her, which had been mostly accidentally after that searing kiss. Heard her breath hitch into that irregular rhythm.

Her artless, instant reaction goaded the devil within him.

"Gabriel?"

He lifted her hand and kissed the center of her palm. Smiling, he let it go when she jerked it back as if scalded. He stood still, used now to the beat of desire in his muscles.

Forced himself to have the patience to wait.

"Fine. I will trust you, *Princesa*. In this, at least."

Any control Eleni thought she had wrested of the situation, of the dynamic between them, disappeared like mist when he held the bottom of his dress shirt and pulled it up over his head in one fluid motion.

Her jaw fell with an audible click. "What... what are you doing?" she croaked out, heat staining her cheeks.

Ropes of leanly defined muscles stretched dark, olive skin. There wasn't an inch of extra flesh on his body. Rubbing a hand over her nape, Eleni was humiliatingly aware of the soft, pillowy cushioning of her own hips and thighs.

Of her unfashionable figure.

Of how her cheeks were plump and her nose far too prominent.

Of how little she had to offer a man like him.

And still, she couldn't unglue her feet from the

floor and walk away. Couldn't say "this is off," even to save her pride.

She stared in fascination as he balled up the shirt and threw it into the corner. Heard the splash of water as he went into the adjoining bathroom.

He came out, water running in rivulets over his naked chest, glistening in the light falling from the windows. He dried the front of his chest, under his arms and around his neck with a towel, all the while holding her gaze with a devilish glint in his own.

"You look flushed, Eleni. Are you unwell?"

Eleni licked her suddenly dry lips, could think of no answer.

He threw the towel into the corner where it joined the shirt. Then he pulled on a fresh white shirt and faced her. His chest gleaming golden brown, he stood in front of her.

Eleni breathed compulsively, the scent of male sweat and cologne making her muscles twitch in response. "What is it that you want of me?"

The most unholy twinkle filled his gray eyes. "Button my shirt."

Eleni stared at the ridge of his chest muscles as the shirt flapped in the soft breeze. Sparse hair covered it, narrowing down into a line below his navel and disappearing into his trousers. Her fingers shook at her sides and she balled them.

Finding the sheer will that had, in the end,

tamed the ferocious man that her father had been, Eleni looked up into Gabriel's eyes. "I have been celibate for too long, Gabriel. It has to be the only reason for this…almost-violent reaction to you. Once I sleep with you, the power won't be in your hands so much." She started toward the door. "Don't keep your daughter waiting any longer," she threw over her shoulder, without turning.

The mocking laughter that followed her stayed with her for nights to come.

Eleni waited in the courtyard for Gabriel, the evening uncommonly cold for autumn.

A flurry of activities had followed the night after she and Gabriel had taken Angelina to see the musical. Father and daughter didn't say much to each other still, except when they argued, but the fact that Gabriel had been present at dinners and every other evening activity Eleni had suggested for the three of them had not been lost on Angelina.

The girl was as stubborn as her father for she didn't ask him for anything. Yet Eleni had seen the anticipation in her eyes that she struggled to hide, the tilt of her chin when she heard her father's voice.

Just as she had seen Gabriel's gaze lingering on Angelina. He had completely shut Eleni down when she'd asked after his sister again. Still, he had given her a lot to mull over.

It was hard to see a different facet of the arrogant businessman, the gorgeous billionaire who had no soft edges. Yet, the fact that his behavior when he'd barely been an adult weighed on him, spoke of a man who had soft edges. Of a man who felt things deeply.

Eleni herself struggled to keep a little rationality about the upcoming wedding. Spending evenings in his company at myriad activities was all well and good for Angelina but not for her own feeble defenses.

Gabriel, she'd learned in the last two weeks, was a charming companion, a humorous storyteller and when the mood stuck him, which was far too often, the very devil himself.

He taunted her senses relentlessly—soft strokes on her wrist, the graze of his body when he sat too close, the dig of his fingers over her shoulders when they posed for a picture at one of his blasted, endless parties. It was as if he was determined to send her over the edge. As if he was determined to punish her for her comment about resisting him.

Somehow, the attraction between them had become a cat and mouse game, and Eleni was alternately thrilled and overwhelmed at being chased by the most powerful, gorgeous man in the world.

She melted under his caresses, despite knowing it was all a game to him. That she was a novelty.

"Get in, *Princesa*."

They were on their way to another one of his parties—something Gabriel insisted she attend when all she wanted to do was hide from the scrutiny.

Coloring at the obvious amusement in his tone, she stepped into the limo and found herself being thoroughly appraised by the devil in front of her. Heat swamped her as he took in the beige silk cocktail dress she had chosen to match the four-inch stilettos that had gold threads winding around her ankles.

Mouth twitching, he kept his gaze on her ankles. Tingles began in her skin as if he had caressed that part with those rough fingers of his. Eleni uncrossed and crossed her ankles, which made her only doubly aware of the slide of the sensitive skin of her thighs. "What?" she demanded finally, her body a thrum of sensations.

"I thought you didn't like heels."

"How do you know that?"

"Angelina asked you when we went to play in the park the other day and you said you felt like you would fall and break your head every time you tried a pair."

Eleni sat back against the soft leather, struggling to hide her reaction. She had no inkling that Gabriel paid any attention to the things she said. And she couldn't help the warmth that stole through her that he did.

He cleared his throat and looked up, a slight rasp in his throat. "Although I must admit I don't think I've ever seen anything quite so sexy—" his eyes gleamed dark in the intimacy of the limo "—I would prefer my fiancée with her head intact for the wedding." He leaned ahead on the seat, his long legs bracing hers on either side, crowding her with that masculinity of his. "Why, Eleni?"

She shrugged. "I felt like a change."

He arrested her with his hands on her wrists when she would have retreated farther into the leather. "How do you think I will give you what you want if you flinch every time I touch you?"

Eleni forced herself to relax, knowing he was right. "I...I'm just not used to constantly being touched. And I wore the damn heels because I'm tired of feeling so short next to you. As if I could forget it, the media reminds me incessantly of how different I am from your usual type."

"But I like how you feel against me, *Princesa*. So fragile and small. My masculinity feels stroked around you."

She snorted. "Your masculinity hardly needs to be stroked, Gabriel."

He threw his head back and laughed.

Like everything he did, even that was sexy. Crinkles spread out from his gray eyes, which danced with humor. "No, I don't think so. But other parts, yes."

Eleni blushed so profusely she felt like there should be flames coming out of her ears.

"Believe me, Princess. Not a single woman I've ever known could match that lovely blush of yours. This modern world of equality has made me unaware of how attractive a woman's shy blushes and stammering denials are."

"I don't stammer," she burst out, efficiently giving herself away.

Anything else she might have vehemently denied died on her lips when his outstretched hand held a small velvet box.

"Open it, Eleni," he said with an edge of impatience after she'd stared it for several seconds.

Eleni slowly opened it and promptly lost her breath.

A sapphire sat in a princess setting surrounded by tiny diamonds that reflected the sun's rays. It was the most exquisite ring she'd ever seen, and as a member of the House of Drakos, Eleni had seen her share.

It wasn't ostentatious with the stone overpowering the setting. It wasn't a status symbol. It wasn't a ring she'd have expected a man like Gabriel Marquez, a man who proclaimed to the world what and who he was with every breath, to buy for his fiancée.

"You do not like the ring."

Eleni closed her fingers over his wrist just as he was about to shut the box. Breath punched in and out of her throat at the graze of the hair on his wrists against her palm.

"It's the most beautiful ring I've ever seen." Breathless and vulnerable. Desperate and so painfully hopeful. Despite every warning that this was just an arrangement, her heart drummed against her rib cage. "I'm trying to rack my brain as to whether I've ever mentioned to any media outlet that sapphires are my favorite."

"I asked your sister-in-law."

She jerked her gaze to his. "You asked Mia?"

He shrugged. "It was actually Angelina's idea. That I get you something you'd like and appreciate. That women want to be given beautiful things. Apparently, I need relationship advice from my twelve-year-old daughter if I want to keep you happy."

Eleni tried to bat away the warmth that immediately flooded her. "It is good that you two have something to discuss. Finally."

"Oh, believe me, my twelve-year-old daughter is not only chock-full of advice but questions too. Even your brothers, I'd say, are not quite the champions of you that Angelina is."

"What do you mean?"

"She demanded to know why I was marrying you while declaring that you deserve someone far better than an unfeeling, workaholic like me."

When he stared at her pointedly, Eleni shook her head. "As much as I hate your guts sometimes, I would never say such a thing about you in front of her. But…"

"Nikandros has no such reservations and Angelina has such a crush on him that everything he says is the truth to her." Eleni nodded with a smile, and he sighed.

"If you start talking about how she's growing up, I'll… I think our conversation about you is the first real one we've ever had. The longest too."

"What did you tell her?"

"Angelina's too smart to be deceived. So I told her one version of truth."

"Which is?"

"That I was thirty-six years old and settling down with a wife wasn't a bad idea, especially if it made her feel secure and loved. That a marriage with shared goals is the only one I could tolerate. That your alleged saintly nature made you the best candidate for the position."

"Saintly nature?"

"Apparently, you're not only a wonderful friend, but also a model sister, daughter, a patroness of children's charities and a superb equestrian." His mouth snarled into a cynical curve that twisted the truth of his words. As if she was somehow cheating the world into believing an illusion. "I was hard-pressed to accept that I deserved to marry such a model of righteousness."

"I'm neither dull nor a saint, Gabriel. The urges I feel when I'm with you will attest to that."

"Like wanting to climb atop me right this minute and ravish me with that lush mouth of yours?"

She sputtered and stammered, not getting one lucid word out for a few seconds. The man was such an inveterate rogue. "Like wanting to thump you every time you use the attraction between us to gain the upper hand."

His languid mouth twitching, he took her hand in his and slipped the ring onto her finger. Eleni's throat felt like it was made of glass as the sapphire winked at her in the low lights of the limousine.

It was for show, she told herself, for the world, for the media, for outward appearances. Yet, it was the first time a man had made a commitment to her and the moment stole what breath was left in her lungs. She gathered her buffeted emotions together as he rubbed her knuckle with his finger, a thoughtful look on his face.

She left her hand in his through sheer effort, her heart racing in her chest. "Thank you, Gabriel. The ring...even if it was Angelina's idea, it's very thoughtful. I know that I'm dragging you to the altar."

"In business, we adhere to the strictest standards because customer satisfaction is the primary goal. Not a profit margin, not whether the next contract lands in your pile. I will do everything in my power to give you everything you want and need, and that will ensure that you will do your best with Angelina. Simple common sense. So tell me, are you dragging me, *Princesa*, or am I dragging you to the altar in two weeks?"

"Two weeks? I'm not even sure whether Andreas got the message I sent. I can't marry without him present."

"I'm a businessman first and foremost. I can't let deals wait for anyone. And you do not need Andreas's blessing when you're the one who's saving Drakon from the big bad wolf. I'm aware how much work there is to be done with Angelina and me, and I will not give you a chance to back out. Andreas is busy chasing a ghost. And anyway, once we marry, Angelina will be your priority, not your brothers."

The ring cold on her finger, Eleni stared at him. Why did she keep forgetting that this was a transaction for him, albeit an important one? He didn't think of her as a woman to woo, only a mother for his daughter.

His cold analysis pinched like the tiniest shard

of glass stuck in one's hand. "Will I be asked to give you a review once you hold up your end of the deal too? Because I would like some kind of scale and advance notice if I'm to rate your…performance."

This time, his laughter only made her feel cold and alone.

She needed to remember that, despite the soft edges she'd seen in him, Gabriel had as much heart as her cold and controlling father. He saw her only as the means to an end.

If she'd been a romantic, then her hopes and dreams would have turned to so much dust by now. Good thing that between her father's cruelty and Spiros's desertion, Eleni had long ago squashed any such hopes.

CHAPTER FIVE

THEIR WEDDING FEAST was held in the Rose room at the Drakon Palace, hosted by his now brother-in-law, Nikandros, and his wife, Mia.

Gabriel took a champagne flute and raised it in a gesture toward him. Nothing, however, could shake that creeping sense that his life was a little less in his control since he and the Princess had come to their neat little arrangement.

In two weeks, she'd made sure he and Angelina had had dinner every night, forced them to at least look at each other. The Princess herself had, of course, been the perfect buffer.

Angelina still had to be dragged to these dinners, he knew, but at least when she got there, she participated in the conversation, especially if Eleni asked her something.

He, who had never believed in anything that defied logic, had to admit that there was something of magic in his bride's eyes when she joined hands with him and smiled up at him with those beautiful brown eyes.

Something beyond the mundane had touched the mountain air when she'd walked toward him on the path carpeted with rose petals. When she had smiled at Angelina who'd been her flower girl with such love shining in her eyes.

He'd had an event management firm do all the preparations for the ceremony, had ordered them to give his fiancée everything she wanted for the wedding, no matter how expensive or outrageous. Only to be told that his fiancée had a very decided opinion of how she wanted her wedding.

Her love for detail shone through in the smallest of touches.

And still, his commitment to this felt like nothing in the face of hers. Like he was cheapening it with his constant reminders that it was only an arrangement between them, with his continued belief that he was only doing this for Angelina, whereas Eleni, once she had decided on the course, seemed to accept it for what it was.

It felt like a weight he hadn't asked for around his chest, a transaction for which her rewards were vague.

A member of his staff joined Gabriel just as Eleni walked onto the dance floor with Nikandros. He barely heard what the man said. Couldn't shake his gaze from the voluptuous beauty of his wife.

His wife—his to cherish and protect and love. He couldn't do the last, but he could surely do the first two.

The ivory lace of her dress dipped in a graceful curve, only barely hinting at those full breasts that his hands tingled to cup and hold.

The delicate diamond tiara sat atop brown curls that fell around her face in teasing waves. It was a gift from her brother Nikandros, Gabriel knew, for she'd refused any jewelry from him. Had smilingly refused every trinket he'd had the jeweler bring up to her.

Only the rings he had put on her finger and the promise of a child.

Even the settlement that Nikandros had insisted she receive in case they separated, had been arranged in their children's names, if they had any.

She didn't want anything Gabriel could give, or wanted to give her, and it made disquiet bloom in his gut that maybe there wasn't anything he could give this woman to balance what she was giving him.

For a man who had measured the world and the people in it in terms of their worth and the value he could provide them, Eleni left him feeling empty-handed.

So Gabriel had smiled and posed for pictures with her and Angelina, even as his skin prickled.

With repeated instructions—almost step-by-step advice on how to approach Angelina and how to overcome her resistance—he and Angelina had even muddled their way through a dance, something he would have called an impossibility even a month ago.

How the media would laugh if they knew how much his own wedding had moved a hardened cynic like him.

He was about to ask Eleni to dance with him again when he saw a tall, tuxedoed man make a bow in front of her. That wide smile slipped from her mouth. Color fled her cheeks, leaving her eyes glittering with tears in a pale mask.

Gabriel frowned, every muscle urging him into action.

She didn't refuse when the man took her hand in his. In fact, a ghost of a smile dawned slowly, a bit hesitant, a bit nervous. Her gaze searched the man's face furiously, as if she couldn't drink him up fast enough. Her hands went to his shoulders, his face, as if she couldn't believe he was there.

A burst of possessiveness filled Gabriel as the man pulled her onto the dance floor, his hands far too bold and familiar over Eleni's figure. Her slender fingers locked against the man's nape, she tilted her head down to his mouth, as if to hear every word.

That look of distress, of disbelief, never left her eyes, all the while she danced with him. Curiosity ate through him, like flames licking at oil. With a curse, Gabriel walked away.

He wasn't going to hang on to his wife's every movement like a jealous husband. Damn it, she wasn't even going to be his wife in the true sense of the word.

CHAPTER SIX

HER NERVES STRETCHED so taut that she felt she might shatter like a piece of glass, Eleni walked the long corridor to her own apartments rather than return to the Rose room. More than two hours had passed since she had disappeared from her own wedding reception with Spiros.

Surely her absence must have been noted by now. She had spent the past half hour trying to make sense of it all, wandering the palace aimlessly, and she didn't have any more clarity.

Spiros—her friend and confidant from her childhood, the only boy she had kissed until Gabriel, the man who had promised to love her for the rest of their lives—was back. After being gone for ten years with no word, message or a single phone call.

Back in her life, apparently, whatever the hell that meant. Finally free to be with her, he'd said. There was no rhyme or reason to the nonsense he had blurted out at her.

A sob fought through her chest and Eleni swallowed hard to lock it. She didn't know what it was that sat like a lump in her throat.

Was it grief? Anger? Or anxiety at what she had left behind in the reception room?

The palace walls seemed to close in on her as she turned one corner after the other. She should have been furious with him. She had imagined for so many years how she would react if she saw him again.

How she would slap his beautiful face and tell him to go to hell. How she would tell him that he had forever crushed her trust in men, her trust in her own judgment and feelings.

She had done none of those things. Her heart seemed to have lodged in her throat, cutting off any chance of words.

It had been such a beautiful day. Almost as if the universe had conspired to make it grand for her. Perfect for her. She'd begun it with a purpose, with a sense of direction for the first time in so many years. And it had ended with a ghost from her past.

Standing in front of the tilted-edge mirror, clad in her ivory lace gown, every inch polished and poised, with a bouquet of rare orchids that Gabriel had sent over, she had felt like a woman reaching for what she wanted out of life.

With the backdrop of the mountain, the chapel had looked like a magical kingdom. Nikandros had told her she'd looked stunning, a reluctant grin on his lips. Had embraced her in a bear hug when she'd mentioned Andreas.

The air had been crisp and pure and the man

waiting for her at the end of the aisle had been the highlight.

Clad in a black tuxedo, his blue-black hair slicked back, he had looked powerful and gorgeous, a most outrageous dream come true. His fingers had been firm on hers, his vows resonating against the very mountain itself.

To protect and honor and cherish he promised in his deep, gravelly voice. She'd wanted to believe every word.

When his lips had touched hers, Eleni had jerked, singed to her very core. Dark brows had drawn down with the same shock she was sure vibrated through her own body.

It was as if their bodies sang to each other, their lips felt that same connection blaze into life even with the barest of contacts.

Her fingers had lingered over his, her face upturned, his for the taking. His mouth had twitched in that satisfied, arrogant way of his and she had blushed to the roots of her hair. But he hadn't deepened the kiss beyond the perfunctory cool slide of his lips over hers.

The ride back to the palace had been filled with chitchat by Angelina. She was a mother in their arrangement, Eleni had reminded herself when Angelina had asked if she could ride with them. Not a proper wife. But even that hadn't dimmed her joy in the day.

Today had been a perfect day she wouldn't soon forget.

Until a suave, smiling Spiros had stood in front of her at the reception, greeting her like a long-lost friend.

Her gut had folded to her feet. She had been so shocked to see him that she had thought him a specter first, a ghost from the past. To remind her of what and who she was, of how naive she could be, how powerful her self-induced delusions if she weren't careful.

When he had taken her arm and pulled her out of the Rose room, she had gone willingly, still grappling with it. When he had held her tight against him, when he had whispered frantic endearments and kissed her hair, she'd frozen into stillness.

Memories she hadn't allowed herself to think of came rushing back, drenching her in pain and sorrow. Spiros had shuddered around her, his greetings shifting to apologies.

And then he'd disappeared as quickly as he had appeared.

Wondering if she was hallucinating, she had roamed the old armory like a wraith, her dress snagging and tearing on a rusted suit.

Her feet hurt like the very devil in her five-inch stilettos.

Leaning against the wall in front of her apartments, she bent and pulled the offending sandals off her feet. All she wanted was to tear her dress off, sink into a bath, and then go to sleep. The sooner morning came, the sooner she could have a bit of her practicality back.

Feet bare, she was pulling at the complicated knot her hair had been twisted into when she saw the shadow of a broad figure saunter into the light of her sitting room.

With the skylights at his back drawing a line around his broad shoulders, Gabriel looked like a devilish creature of the night. A darkly commanding figure. His suit jacket was gone. His white dress shirt unbuttoned and pulled out of his trousers. The edges separated to display a rockhard chest with olive skin stretched tight.

A glass of scotch, his preferred drink, shone amber in his hands as he filled the doorway, lazily leaning a hip against it. His gaze started at her bare feet that she scrunched against the cold marble, traveled up the tulle skirt, lingered far too long on her hips and breasts and then up her bare neck, toward the hair she had partially pulled free of the knot.

Every inch of her tingled at his lazily possessive perusal. At the banked fire gleaming to life in his gray gaze. Every muscle in her tightened consciously against the onslaught of heat he created with that one long look.

Her sandals fell from her fingers with a quiet

thud that resonated with the fierce drumming of her heart. She'd been so consumed with shock over Spiros that she'd even forgotten what tonight meant.

Did he mean to consummate their wedding tonight?

Shock and something more sinuous slowly floated down into her consciousness, setting off tremors in her entire body.

Did she want to refuse him?

No, came her body's resounding answer. Not when she'd been through nervousness, excitement and every other emotion anticipating this one night. Not when it felt like she'd waited for this, for him, her entire life. Would he be gentle or would that hardness she'd sensed in him spill over to their personal intimacies?

But seeing Spiros had sent her on a strange spiral, as if the rug had been pulled from under her feet just when she was finding safe ground. Thoughts and questions about the past filled her to the brim so that her present, this man in front of her, felt like a stinging slap. As if she had brought a shadow into this fresh, new life of theirs.

He took a swig of his drink while she watched and wiped his mouth roughly. "Do you plan to undress right there in the corridor, *querida*?"

Silky as it sounded, Eleni didn't miss the vein of steel beneath his question. "No." When he didn't move, she tried to take stock of her situation. "I…I'm sorry I didn't realize you'd be here tonight." She sounded so lame to her own ears that she cringed.

"Where would a bridegroom be on his wedding night? Or is it not time for me to hold up my side of the bargain yet?"

Eleni gripped her elbows with her hands as if she could ward off the humiliating hurt that pinged through her.

One man had deserted her years ago without a word and one was bent on punishing her for something she hadn't done. Tears made her voice unbearably soft, almost fragile.

"Is my desire for a child so cheap in your eyes, Gabriel? Or is it that you can't force yourself to perform in the bounds of a marriage?"

"I'm not the one who decided to disappear without a word. Imagine my surprise, however, when neither Angelina nor your brother nor I could locate you for well over two hours. Your phone was off, Eleni," he bit out, "and even I know that that thing is almost surgically attached to you."

"I must have left it somewhere in all the rush."

"Even your aide could not locate you."

Her head jerked up as she realized the truth of his hard mouth, the granite jaw. The deceivingly slumbering stare and the poisonous barbs.

He was angry with her. Blazingly furious. Not

even on the night of the masquerade ball had he been like this. A shiver wrapped its fist around her spine. "Gabriel, are you angry with me?"

The question seemed to take him back. As if he hadn't quite realized it himself. "I'm merely confused, *Princesa*. You disappeared from the reception for two hours, and then you appear outside your apartments, close to midnight, your hair unraveled, your dress almost falling apart at the seams and I have to confess to wondering what the mystery is."

Eleni tugged the torn sleeve of her dress against her neck hastily and then realized the futility of the action. He'd drawn his conclusions already.

She pushed her hair from her brow, searching for some suitable story. She couldn't just admit the humiliating truth. Couldn't bear to see the cynicism in his eyes when she told him of how Spiros had disappeared from her life and how she had hung on for years before finally giving up.

The scorn in his eyes at her supposed naïveté.

A stillness claimed him as he correctly read her guilty silence. "I'm waiting for an explanation, *Princesa*."

"I saw an old friend," she said, wanting to stick to the truth as much as possible. "We started catching up and completely lost track of time. I—"

"Is this friend a man?"

Drawing her arms around her neck, she shook

her head. "No." The moment the word left her mouth, she wanted to snatch it back. "She...I hadn't seen her in a long time and it was a shock to see her today, that's all."

"You didn't invite...this friend to the wedding?"

"Her sister used to work here at the palace and she decided to surprise me." Lie after lie fell from her mouth and she could not stop them. But what else could she say?

That the man she'd once desperately loved had returned after ten years of being gone on her wedding day? Or that he had held her as if his heart was breaking? Or that he'd promised her in an almost-hysterical whisper that he would never again leave her?

"Why is your dress torn?"

She lifted her chin defiantly, a slow burn of anger washing away the guilt. "What is it that you think I have done, Gabriel?"

"No groom wants to be disenchanted with his bride on their wedding night, does he?" Silken mockery dripped from his every word, making a lie of everything the day had represented.

"I told you before. I'm neither a saint nor as dull as they make me out to be," she snarled back, frustration and guilt coiling into a rope within her.

He shrugged and the movement bared one dark nipple. "Angelina said to say good-night. She insisted on waiting for you, but I finally was able to persuade her to go to bed."

The knot in her stomach twisted some more. She felt like she was on a swing of emotions, going high and low on guilt and regret and anger. All because the one man she'd desperately needed was ten years late, and the man she had promised herself to in his place now stared at her as if she had betrayed him on the very eve of their wedding.

For the rigid set of his mouth and the hard look in his eyes said what he wouldn't voice. "I'm sorry. I completely—"

"Lost track of everything, you said. Despite the fact that Angelina worries unnecessarily when people disappear all of a sudden. You know, after her mother's accident and all."

A mewl of regret fell from her mouth. She knew what Angelina suffered having seen the panic in her eyes when her dog had been missing one afternoon. "You're beating a dog that's already down," she whispered. "I already said I'm sorry. Nothing is more important to me than the fact that Angelina feels safe and loved."

Gaze intent on her face, he nodded. "And the worry you put me through, *querida*?"

Her gaze jerked to his. He had to be joking. "You worried about me?"

"Yes. Until now you were just the Princess

of Drakon, mostly ignored, working behind the scenes, blending into the palace walls, but now—"

"That's not true," she protested, slow anger burning in her chest.

He pushed off from the wall, dropped his glass onto a side table and neared her. "Now you are Gabriel Marquez's wife. There will be unwanted attention. There will be media curiosity. Whatever you do, there will be someone with a phone or a camera around."

The scent of him filled her nostrils. One long finger reached out and traced the seam of her torn sleeve, drawing a line of fire against her bare shoulder. He radiated such warmth that Eleni thought she would go up in flames. "One chance, *Princesa*. You have one chance to tell me where you were."

Her cheeks flushed with heat but Eleni gazed back at him steadily. "Nothing has happened that warrants this kind of questioning from you."

His head tilted. His disbelief stood between them like the wall of a fortress, crumbling the tenuous connection they had made with each other the past few weeks. He was again that ruthless stranger who didn't trust her at all.

"Now, should I tell you something I have been wanting to say all day to you?"

She nodded, not trusting herself to speak. Not trusting the dangerous glint in his eyes. Not trusting the sharp craving of her own body.

Spine stiff against the wall, she licked her dry lips. His gray gaze zoomed in on the movement. Hands on the wall over her head, he leaned forward until their bodies grazed. Such honed power filled him, such heat emanated from him that she was drawn toward him with every breath, against her own will.

With a flick of his finger, he pushed the torn sleeve aside. Traced the intimate fold of her arm, the rising curve of her pushed-up breast.

Then while he held her gaze with his, he bent and pressed his mouth to the bared flesh.

Eleni gasped low in her throat.

The flick of his tongue sent a molten spark to the flesh between her legs. An ache throbbed into life there and she clenched her thighs tight to hold it off, to stop from falling into the sexual miasma of his presence.

"I have wanted to rip that gown off you from the moment you walked toward me. But since you gave that pleasure to—"

"A suit of old armor did it, Gabriel," she said huskily, desperate for the coldness in his eyes to abate.

"To someone else, I will settle for having you in my bed tonight. I will have to settle with knowing that it will be me moving inside you, *Princesa*."

"I—"

And before she could respond to that sultry

statement, he closed his mouth over the flesh he had licked. And sucked it between his teeth.

Head banging hard against the wall, Eleni let out a low sound. Pleasure exploded inside her body. The graze of his lips moved to the upper swell of her breast while his hands molded the dip of her waist, the flare of her hips. "You were made to be loved, *Princesa*. This body, every whimper and moan that comes out of your mouth...they belong to me."

Rough hands rucked her dress up and up until his palm pressed between her clenched thighs. "Let me in, Princess," he uttered roughly.

But her legs were already spreading of their own accord, making a space for him at the innermost core of her.

The slide of his abrasive palms over the tender skin of her inner thighs, the stroke of his hot breath over her neck, the way he had pressed her into the wall with his hard body—Eleni was in heaven and hell.

The sensory input was too much, her body breathing hard to play catch-up.

She wanted to beg him to go slow, to give her a second to get used to the invasive intimacy of his caresses, but she was new to this sharp pleasure, was floating away in it and the required words would not form.

His palm covered her mound and her breath hissed out of her in uneven jerks.

"Your hair glints like burnished gold, *Princesa*. Are you the same here?" Wicked whispers brushed against her swelling flesh, while his fingers boldly opened her up for his exploration. "Shall I kiss you here, Eleni?" One finger dipped inside of her and she arched against him. She had never been so aware of her flesh there, tight and throbbing. Wet and aching.

Then he rubbed a finger over the swollen hood crying for his touch.

Shivers bunched in her muscles making her fevered and achy all over. She tried to reach for him but he was far too strong as he caged her in place with his body. When he flicked that bundle with deft, continual strokes, all breath left Eleni.

"Please, Gabriel..."

His mouth moved over the swell of her breast, toward the achy center that had hardened into a knot. "I shall make you as crazy as you did me today, Eleni. I shall make you beg."

A sharp cry left her as he tore the bodice and closed his mouth over her nipple. "Oh..." Eleni bit her lip hard. It was the only way to stop herself from begging.

"I warned you, Eleni. I abhor lies and deceit."

The bitter anger in his words barely registered on the sensual haze that filled her mind and body.

Stretched taut against the wall, Eleni lost her grip on her will.

Moans and whimpers fell from her mouth, erotic sounds that seemed to fuel her husband's dark demands of her.

His strokes deepened in speed and rhythm until she was riding his hand, grinding her wanton flesh against his palm with a madness she had never known.

His wicked lips pulled at her sensitized nipples while his fingers set a punishing rhythm she couldn't fight. He let the sensitive flesh go with a popping sound that vibrated in tune with the throb at her core. Teeth digging into his shoulder, Eleni sobbed as pleasure splintered in her lower belly and poured through her muscles in deep, clenching spasms.

Turned inside out, she felt raw, utterly spent.

She fell onto him like a rag doll, shattered and bare, tears crowding her throat.

The most intense, earth-shattering experience of her life and he had given it to her in anger. Ice frosted her heart even as tendrils of heat filled her muscles.

While she was still trembling, her heart thundering in her chest, while her muscles were still struggling to return from that heightened state, his hands moved to her thighs and he picked her up, as if she were a china doll.

Pressed against the granite wall of his chest, her breasts felt sore, heavy. Sleep battered her in waves and Eleni struggled to stay afloat.

She'd triggered some emotional reaction in this hard man. Yet the woman in her caved to the man in him, to the masculine possessiveness with which he carried her off. To the deep want etched in the strong planes of his face.

No one had ever wanted her like that. No one had ever shown her a hundredth of the emotion he showed. But even through the lingering waves of her climax, she knew he didn't trust her, that whatever this was between them, it was far from what she'd imagined for them.

When he threw her onto his bed, she tried to move back and tangled her legs in her own dress. When she tried it again, his hand held on to the edge of her skirt. The loud rip of the fabric punctured the sensual web.

Heart thudding, Eleni looked up. "Gabriel?" She said his name, half surrender, half retreat.

Masculine challenge glinting in his eyes, Gabriel leaned his torso toward her. His rough hands crawled up her skirt, on top of it. Knees, thighs, belly, the hollow between her breasts, his broad palm touched her everywhere.

Need coiled deeper and tighter in her again, for this time she knew what he could give her. Her body was desperately eager for another explosion.

Somehow Eleni found the sense to still his hands when they reached the bodice.

"Wait, Gabriel," she whispered, the words coming as if through a long tunnel, as if from a rational mind disjointed from the yearning desires of her body.

He sat at her feet, every inch of his rugged face taut and rigid. "Ah…I did not take you for a tease, Eleni."

Sweat beaded her forehead, her body unwilling to let go of him. Through sheer will, Eleni pushed herself onto her elbows. Her dress billowed around her legs as she leaned her forehead against his shoulder.

He stiffened, his fingers pushing at her shoulders.

She clasped his bristly jaw willing him to listen. "I don't want our first night together to be spent in doubt and mistrust. I don't want a child conceived like this."

"We have nothing but that, *Princesa*. You'll never have a child if you want us to come together in some sort of transcendent emotion that doesn't exist."

"Don't say that."

"All we have is this mindless lust."

"Because I angered you?"

He pressed the heel of his hand to his eyes, and then sighed. Resignation in his gray eyes pierced deeper than his anger. "Because you lied, Eleni. Because you proved that for all the moral pedestal you stand on, you're just like every other woman on the planet. That you're what I thought you that first night."

"What are you talking about?"

He shook a phone in her face. A sick feeling climbed up her throat as he pressed Play. A clip of Spiros and her played like a reel from some ghastly nightmare.

Whoever had shot it should be given a prize, Eleni thought hysterically, for they had shot them from the side. His gaze devouring her, Spiros held her still form in his arms so tight that no one could doubt the meaning of it. He was frantic, almost mad as he ran his hands over her body.

It looked like a lover's caresses, and yet she knew in her heart, he hadn't touched her like that at all.

Bile filled Eleni's mouth as he pressed fevered kisses all over her face all the while muttering things no one could hear. But the shock in her face, that was not visible.

The clip seemed to go on interminably until Eleni grabbed the phone from Gabriel and threw it across the room.

"Gabriel, listen to me. It's not like that at all. Spiros and I—"

Gabriel stood up from the bed, his face set into

cold lines. "You had your chance. Now that I have your measure, I feel better about this whole arrangement. To think I felt guilty that you deserved better! That you were being cheated out of everything in this stupid arrangement. Of course you have a nice little lover on the side. Now I see why you were so ready to sacrifice yourself on the altar of Drakon."

Eleni pushed back from him, the depth of his bitterness like a stinging slap against her flesh. "Gabriel, you make me sound positively Machiavellian." A bitter laugh fell from her mouth. "It is no wonder you couldn't forge a bond with Angelina, is it? You have nothing but a stone for a heart. Nothing but poison filling your veins."

Utter frost dawned in his eyes as he stepped away from her. As if she had contaminated him. "I don't give a damn who you cavort with…but one word of it reaches the press, one word of your duplicity reaches Angelina's ears, you will regret the day you walked into my life."

CHAPTER SEVEN

WARM SUNLIGHT KISSED Eleni's face when she opened her eyes. An achy awareness pulsed between her legs. The sheets seemed to caress her very skin; she'd never felt such delicious languor.

The smile fell from her face as the events of the past night came back to her. She ran the back of her hand over her eyes and came away with smudges from her mascara and tears, she was sure. If not for the unfamiliar awareness between her legs, she'd have thought the whole thing a bad dream.

But Spiros had stolen her away from her own wedding reception. And Gabriel had known and been furious about it.

Eleni sat up in her bed and rubbed her eyes with a groan. Thoughts came and went, like pictures in a kaleidoscope. And suddenly she saw things with a clarity that had been lacking last night. How could she have seen clearly when Gabriel's barbs had wounded her so deep?

But why had he been so angry, so irrational? Why, when he'd always seemed so uncaring, so blasé about their impending nuptials?

She'd expected anger, yes, even his derision. But his reaction had been personal, as if she had somehow disappointed him? As if she had hurt him?

She snorted and cursed herself. As if anything she did or didn't do could affect the blasted man.

And the video... Christos, she wanted to slap whoever had shot it and quietly handed it to Gabriel.

In fact, she wanted to give a piece of her mind to all of them—the imbecile who had sneaked up on her and shot it; Spiros, who'd been half-delirious; ending with her husband, who blew hot and cold in the space of a minute.

Was it his ego that had been bruised or had Gabriel truly wanted her with that craving she'd seen in his eyes last night?

Was it her he didn't trust?

Or women in general?

Would she be left in a limbo once again, tied to a man who didn't want her, but now spoken for? Married but never a wife?

Mother to Angelina but not even the possibility of another child?

The darker her thoughts went, the tighter her throat became until she was angry with herself.

Self-pity had never solved anything for her.

She pushed away the duvet and got to her feet. Ordering a coffee, she quickly brushed her teeth, washed up. When breakfast arrived, she ordered it to be arranged on her balcony.

From up here, she had a view of the beautiful gardens that Mia tended to and the riot of color there pushed her spirits up. She grabbed her tablet and began to make a list of things she had to accomplish that day. Nothing was unconquerable as long as she was in action.

First, she'd have to make sure Angelina wasn't still upset over yesterday.

Second, she'd have to see if Mia needed any help.

Then, she'd have to check with Nik and see if he'd heard anything from Andreas.

Sighing, she continued to add items to the list—at this rate it would be at least a year before she could approach Gabriel again—and finished her coffee.

A staff member brought her a white envelope. Reaching for it, she frowned. "What is it?"

"One of the palace staff said it was given to her by a man and asked to be specifically given to you."

Eleni thanked her and opened the note inside.

Eleni,

I'm sorry for frightening you like that. But seeing you as another man's bride was torture for me, *pethi mou*. I saw the same shock and hope in your eyes.

This time no one will separate us. This time I intend to claim you for my own. Neither your brothers nor your husband scare me. Not anymore.

Wait for me, my love.

Yours,
Spiros

Cold sweat trickled down her nape stealing the warmth of the sun.

Why was Spiros writing to her like this? What the hell did he mean no one could separate them this time? Did he think she was anything but shocked out of her mind to see him?

She needed to talk to him. Find out why he had left her like that last time. Find out why he thought she would welcome him with open arms when he hadn't had the decency to approach her for so many years.

It was only in the past two years that she'd finally looked to the future. Only with Andreas's help, even before her father's death, that she'd realized that she didn't have to spend her life grieving over a man who hadn't looked back.

And just when she had reached for a future, there was Spiros.

The shock of seeing him yesterday now gave way to other questions.

Why now? Why was he writing to her like this? Where had he been and what did he want from her? And why was it all cloaked in such mystery?

Annoyed beyond measure, she tore the letter into small pieces. Found a vicious satisfaction in the childish act.

She added "Move On" to her bullet points and sighed. If only it were as easy as that.

A long shadow fell on her tablet blocking her view and Eleni looked up.

"Move on from what?"

His gravelly voice played a chord in that place between her thighs. Steady heat climbed up Eleni's cheeks.

Dressed in black trousers and a long-sleeved gray shirt that made his eyes gleam doubly, Gabriel was watching her. His jaw was clean shaven, his hair wet and slicked back.

Belatedly, Eleni moved her hand over her tablet. "That list is private."

Her breath left her afresh as the breeze carried the scent of soap and skin from him to her.

Ruggedly masculine and gorgeous, he made her mouth dry and her heart ache in her chest. The platinum ring she had placed on his unfamiliar finger gleamed bright in the sun.

A symbol of their relationship, of his commitment to her. She looked down at her own hand and her own ring. The sapphire winked at her, mocking her.

So much for thinking he was much more approachable and easygoing than her father or her older brother, Andreas. "Is there something you needed?" she said, determined to be civil.

His gaze stayed somewhere on her shoulder so she tilted her own head to see what. Her silk robe had slipped off her shoulder, and the morning sun showed the startling bruise his mouth had left on the upper swell of her breast.

Eleni blushed furiously just as his fingers circled her nape and tugged her closer. When the pad of his thumb moved over the purple mark, a sliver of pain made her gasp. A shard of pleasure shot through to her core, making her damp.

Pain and pleasure, he'd given her both yesterday. He hadn't been able to help himself, she realized now, as she felt the solid strength of him surround her. The idea of a helpless Gabriel, a Gabriel who was a slave to his need for her—it unleashed a sense of power that she'd never quite known.

Was she being delusional yet again?

When she leaned into him just so that the tip of her breasts brushed his muscular arm, she felt the faint shudder that traversed his huge body. Mirth bubbled up in her chest.

He was not immune to her, she realized with unabashed curiosity. He didn't trust her, he didn't want to want her, but this gorgeous, powerful man did want her. Suddenly, the dynamic between them was more fluid. Less absolute.

Like she too had a say in where this convenient marriage of theirs went. Was that why his reaction had been so out of character? "Gabriel," she finally said, locking her fingers around his wrist. Tension filled his body, permeating through to her.

"I did that?" he asked, his voice male and low.

Her temper flared. "Yes, just as it was you who put me in a temper, Gabriel. Not the man in the video."

A blank mask fell over the expression in his eyes again. With such thick lashes, no wonder she could never make out what he was thinking. "I apologize."

"For thinking I had gone to bed with another man in the hours between the reception and our wedding night? Or for taking that as a challenge and proving that you could still seduce me? Did it soothe your ego to know that you have that power over me? Is it that old 'I don't want you but my ego will chafe if you so much as look at another man' thing?"

Gabriel blanched, knowing that every word out of her mouth was true. He didn't have an excuse for his behavior.

Even in the corrosive anger that filled him at the thought of that video, he had been a beast to her. He had seduced her, brought her to that raw precipice of pleasure just to prove that she was putty in his hands.

She had called him on it too. The depth of his own bitterness when he'd always breezed through his relationships with women disconcerted him.

Maybe because he'd fallen for the act. Maybe he'd assumed her to be a saint, just because she was such a good mother figure to Angelina.

Maybe the damned woman had got beneath his skin.

Whatever it was, he had never lost control of himself like that. Never had his emotions been in such a riot.

Cheeks flushed with sleep, hair mussed, she looked like a red-blooded male's wet dream. As if all her beauty had needed to bloom into such voluptuousness was a man's touch. His touch.

Even now, all he wanted was to pull her to him and kiss her. To taste her mouth that trembled in such anger. To strip that flimsy robe and night-gown from her body and see the glory of her full curves in sunlight. To mark her again and again until she was covered in the scent of him. Until she forgot every other man.

"I have no excuse for my behavior," he finally said, meeting her soft gaze. "I should not have laid a finger on you last night."

Her shoulders fell on a long exhale. The lines of her face softened and she looked up at him. Her skin glowed with that golden sheen but there were dark shadows under her intelligent eyes. "Since you're determined to be bloody-minded, it falls to me to be the sensible one. To explain."

Gabriel wanted to leave. To not delve further into the woman who was clearly messing with his head. To keep their arrangement strictly platonic, her demands be damned. And yet, he was aware that he would not.

That the identity of that blasted man in that video and what he meant to her would haunt him, leaving him useless for anything else.

"I did give you a chance, *Princesa*. You lied."

Pink filled her sun-kissed cheeks. She licked her lips, looked up and her eyes widened at whatever she saw in his gaze. He didn't care what. A low hum had already begun in his muscles as he took in the silken way her nightgown clung to her curves.

God, she'd been a dream in his hands last night.

"I...I was in shock." She sat down and looked at her fisted hands in her lap. "I hadn't seen him in ten years. For a minute there on the dance floor, I thought him a ghost."

"You had more than two hours for your heart-warming reunion, *Princesa*. Two hours to process it."

"Have you never hidden something humiliating from others, Gabriel? Or were you born like this—invulnerable and hard-hearted?"

"Tell me about him, Eleni. And the truth this time."

A ghost of a smile touched her mouth, as though the memory of him pulled it from her. "Spiros was a ray of light in my life. He...never judged me for my birth. He made me laugh. He told me he loved me for myself, not for what I could mean to him. Or who I was connected to. Before I had formed a bond with Andreas or even Nikandros, Spiros was there, always ready with a laugh and a joke.

"He...used to tell me I was the most genuine person he'd ever met." Another smile. Another thread of that wistfulness in her voice. As if she'd lost something infinitely precious. "That he couldn't help loving me. He was a shoulder to cry on when my father's cruelty was too much to bear. When I felt like I was stuck between Andreas's cold control and Nikandros's impulsive defiance and couldn't lose either. When I felt like nothing I did would ever make me different from who I was. Spiros made me feel wanted. Just for myself."

"What happened then?" he cut in harshly, infuriated that his own heart was racing.

"On my nineteenth birthday, he asked me to marry him. I said yes. He kissed me in the courtyard garden, said he would speak to my father the next day. That's the last I saw of him."

"What do you mean?"

"I mean that I didn't see him again until he appeared at the reception last night. It was like he had disappeared into the night. For years, I thought he had met with some unfortunate accident. Andreas inquired with his family and found out recently that Spiros had just upped and left for the States. They didn't know anything about me or that he'd proposed. I...I just couldn't believe he was back. I went when he asked if we could talk, and I stood there, still in shock, when he hugged me and kissed me.

"When I returned to our suite, there you were. Even if I had told you the truth, you wouldn't have believed me, Gabriel. You already believed the worst."

He had. He did. Until now, he hadn't realized how much his own mother's lies had stayed with him. "Do you love him?"

It was the last question Eleni expected him to ask, this husband of hers who had reminded her again and again that he thought every emotion was a weakness. That he didn't believe in marriage, much less love.

That theirs was a cold, clinical arrangement.

"I loved him years ago. With every breath in me. I believed that he and I...we could be truly happy. Greeting card happy."

"Greeting card happy?" He looked so nauseated that Eleni laughed.

"Like Mia and Nikandros," she said, and looked away.

Suddenly, she felt his fingers under her chin, the rough dig of his thumb onto her jaw. His hard gaze held hers, as if he wanted to plumb the depths of her soul. As if he could will her into giving the answer he wanted. Which was what?

What did Gabriel want? All her confusion about Spiros misted when she gazed into his gray eyes, when she felt his gaze on her.

"You haven't answered my question, *Princesa*. Do you love this man?"

Faint tension filled his frame. Something inside her goaded Eleni, something she'd never felt before. "Would you let me go if I did?"

"No." The word was like a detonation between them, a gauntlet thrown down. Eleni shivered under his touch, aware that his interest in her was personal. She didn't know how but she knew it and it sent a thrill of excitement and fear through her. "If you leave our marriage now, if you turn your back on Angelina, I will—"

"Yes, yes, you will sink Drakon, you will raze the house of Drakos to the ground etc. etc. Really, Gabriel, your threats are becoming tiresome. I have never walked away from a promise I have made."

He continued to stare at her, as if he didn't quite believe her. This matter of trust between them had to be dealt with. Their being at each other's throat like last night could only hurt Angelina, or any other children they had.

He had listened to her—that had to be enough for now.

That he was attracted to her filled her with a rare sense of feminine power that she'd never known. When he stood up to walk away, she looked up at him. They had crossed some line in their relationship. That awareness tingled in the very air about them.

And Eleni was far too confused by her own reaction to question his right now. Too scared to ask what he wanted of her. "I came to tell you that I'm appointing security personnel to guard you. It's a measure your brothers should have taken long ago."

Hurt splintered through her. "Is that for my protection or for spying on me?"

He shrugged, and for the first time since they had met, he was the one that looked away. Tension tightened around his mouth. "As my wife, you need the protection," he said, and walked away.

Leaving her question about trust unanswered. But at least he'd called her his wife.

Leaving her claimed, even though he hadn't touched her again.

* * *

Eleni looked around the huge bedroom with satisfaction. The staff had unpacked most of her stuff and put it away in Gabriel's bedroom. A thrill shot through her as she walked into the stadium-sized closet. When Gabriel had arrived in Drakon, he'd only been a guest of the palace, and yet he'd been given one of the best apartments. His company was a billionaire investor in Drakon, and Nikandros had wanted no deficiency in their hospitality.

Eleni herself had chosen this apartment for him. It afforded a gorgeous view of the mountains in the distance on one side and the ocean on the other. The best of Drakon's views for Gabriel Marquez.

But in seven months, nothing had changed in the suite. No photo frames adorned the side table, not even a picture of Angelina. No keepsakes of his family.

With a frown, she remembered Gabriel hadn't known of the little girl's existence until a few months ago.

She could imagine his wrath that Angelina's mother had hidden such a big truth from him. But beneath that, she wondered now, did he feel betrayal too? Had it perhaps skewed his perception of women? Did he think all women would betray him given the smallest chance?

She had received two more notes from Spiros and she had torn them both up without even opening them. He was in her past; Gabriel was her future.

She'd decided to give him no thought unless he showed himself to her. Unless he stopped playing these silly games with her.

In the meantime, she was determined to sort out her marriage, whatever it took. Gabriel might not want her as his wife but he was attracted to her. They had to move past the impasse they seemed to be at—their relationship was neither the calculated arrangement they initially thought, nor was it going forward.

Beneath the hardness and cold demeanor, there was a man with integrity. A man who loved his daughter, hard though he found it to express it. A man who'd had shown her in three weeks of marriage that he was charming, funny and loyal to those he considered his.

A man who looked at Eleni like she was the tastiest morsel he'd ever seen.

A man who grunted and grumbled when Eleni offered him advice about Angelina but followed it because he wanted his daughter to be happy.

A man who took on Nikandros because he thought she was being taken advantage of by her brothers.

She liked her husband, she realized, running her hands over the sheets. Gabriel's scent—musky and something of the sea—sent acute longing threading through her.

She wanted a proper life with him and Angelina. Even with his sidelong glances—sometimes fuming, sometimes so hot that she thought she'd sizzle on the spot—the last three weeks had been the happiest she'd known in a long time. Maybe ever.

Throat full, she straightened a few ties in the closet.

It was the sense of belonging he'd given her, she knew. With Gabriel and Angelina, she had a place. Father and daughter—while negotiating a tenuous truce between each other—had made Eleni feel invaluable to them. Made her feel wanted.

She'd do anything to make that permanent.

She'd just have to prove to him that this marriage and this life she shared with him and Angelina was everything to her.

Respect and loyalty and belonging—it was more than she'd ever expected.

She reached for her tablet, opened her to-do list and added an item.

Seducing Gabriel would be more than a bullet point in her list soon.

"Are you and Ellie fighting, Papa?"

The question zoomed out of Angelina's mouth while Gabriel was finishing up the designs for the last mountain resort his company was building in Drakon.

He ripped up the blueprint in front of him and wadded it into a pulp. Restlessness like he'd never known filled him, marring the pleasure he had always found in his work. The pleasure he'd found in making money, or in a sexy woman.

Nothing satisfied him anymore.

Nothing he had done over the last few weeks had distracted his mind from the warm woman he found in his bed every night when he returned to his bedroom.

When he had snarled at Eleni and asked if there wasn't a spare room in the entire damn palace, the minx had looked at him serenely and said she hadn't wanted to give any of the staff a chance to gossip about them.

She'd also pointed out that "wasn't the entire reason he had married her to provide Angelina with a secure, home atmosphere? The security of knowing that there wasn't just one but two people who cared about her?"

Of course, having never shared a suite, much less a bedroom with a woman, Gabriel had no idea what he had signed up for.

Day after day, his damn wife's "stuff" crept all over the apartment, taking up space. If he reached for a shirt, there was her yellow dress that had made her look like a voluptuous sunflower.

If he reached for his cuff links, there was her jewelry case filled with the funky costume jewelry she apparently loved collecting.

If, after a long day at work, he went in for a shower, there she was in the giant tub, filled with frothy bubbles and a hundred candles playing peekaboo with damp, soft flesh he wanted to caress, bare thighs he wanted to kiss.

He was the real estate billionaire and even his bathroom was not his own.

The pocket-sized minx was driving him so insane that any given minute he either wanted to throttle her or kiss her senseless.

The only reason he hadn't stalked out of those apartments was now standing behind him.

Calling him *papa* without even realizing she was doing it.

Whatever torment Eleni was causing his flesh—and he worried he was going to be walking with a permanent hard-on—Gabriel grinned and bore it, for Angelina had bloomed like anything in the last weeks. The sparkle in his daughter's eyes every day, the transformation from a sullen child to a lovely, cheerful girl was amazing.

Clearly, his wife knew what she was talking about.

"If you are busy, Papa," came the tentative voice again, "I'll return later."

"No, stay, *querida*," he replied softly.

Willing the tension in his muscles to ease, swallowing away the urge to snarl, as he'd been doing at everyone else, Gabriel put his pencil down and turned.

Her dark hair bound in a tight braid and clad in a white shirt and jodhpurs, Angelina looked like a little champion. "Had a good riding lesson?" he asked, signaling her to come into his office.

After a reluctant minute, she slowly entered. He smiled for the first time in days. Like him, his daughter was a very calculating sort of person. In every interaction between them, he could almost see her weighing the risks and advantages.

Wondering if he could be trusted. And yet, if Eleni had been present, she wouldn't have hesitated even barging in.

"It was a good lesson, although Ellie didn't join us."

"Oh?" he said, striving to keep his voice casual. For one thing, he hadn't known that Eleni was joining Angelina during her riding lessons, although he couldn't say he was surprised.

Apparently, among all her numerous talents, his wife was a superb equestrian. He hadn't yet seen her ride but Angelina couldn't stop talking about it.

It also hadn't taken him long to realize that Eleni was a very hands-on person, even when it came to matters of Angelina. Nothing was trivial enough—not Angelina's education, not her outfits, not even shopping and ice-cream trips were delegated to a nanny or an assistant. Yet, he was also aware that she'd shed none of her other duties.

Since Nik's wife, Mia, was late into her pregnancy with twins and damn Andreas was still MIA, Eleni was playing hostess for Nikandros for many of the state functions of Drakon.

While he grumbled about her taking up space in his suite, the quiet in those rooms when she was out on the social whirl or some palace affair had become unbearable.

Perversely, it bothered him that she had a full life without him when he should be glad that she hadn't made any demands of him again. That he had acquired a mother for Angelina without having to make any emotional investment.

So why did he feel as though slowly but surely the Princess was winning a game he hadn't even realized they were playing? Why did he sometimes catch her gaze on him with such stark yearning in it, the same deep, visceral need he felt when he found her scrunched up tight on one side of his bed?

She rarely came to bed before him and she was dressed and breakfasting on the veranda with her tablet in hand when he woke up. Gabriel had seen the evidence of her hard work in the bruised shadows under her eyes, in the sunken tightness of her features.

If she didn't slow down, Eleni would work herself into an early grave. Yet the woman had a stubborn will that no one could shake.

"So, tell me, are you two fighting?" Angelina prodded.

"Didn't you ask her the same question?" he said, tugging on her braid.

As had become a habit between them, she swatted his hand away first. But then didn't let go completely.

As if she needed the guise of that slap to touch him.

"You growl and grumble like a grumpy giant, Gabriel. Of course it took her time to become familiar with your...physicality."

"Is that why you flinch every time I touch you?" he'd asked Eleni, falling into the lure of those wide, fluttering eyes.

"Why don't you touch me now and see?" the minx had taunted him.

The Princess had become bold. Just like his daughter, there was always a sparkle in her eyes, a spring in her step. It was strangely exhilarating to see Eleni come into her own as a mother.

She'd be a fierce lioness, a great mother to any of their children. The errant thought dropped into his head like a small explosive.

With a muffled curse, he ran his fingers through his hair. If he took her, and every cell in his body wanted to, Gabriel knew he was making a deeper commitment. It could never be a convenient arrangement. He already couldn't bear the thought of another man with her, much less touching her or kissing her. And if he did, he couldn't just move on to another woman.

It was not the example he wanted to set for his daughter. And more than that, it was not what the Princess deserved.

So what the hell was he then signing on for? A true marriage? A relationship with respect and loyalty she already had from him, so was this about passion? God forbid, emotion?

"Papa, you're not listening."

Falling to his knees, which he knew she liked, Gabriel made an apologetic face. "Sorry, *Tesoro*."

"Anyway, I wanted to ask Ellie if you and she were fighting. She's been a little quiet this past week and to be honest, I think she's very sad," she said with the stunning perception of a child. "I went to see her yesterday afternoon and she... she wasn't feeling well. So I wanted to ask if you were the reason and to tell you to lay off."

"Lay off?" he said, his mouth twitching at the fierceness of her tone.

"Yes, lay off. I think she's already in shock

about her old friend. As strong as Ellie is, it's a lot of people to worry over."

His interest perking up, Gabriel casually said, "Old friend?"

"I heard Nik and her talking about it. She was crying and he held her and said he was sorry. I have never seen her like that."

A jolt went through Gabriel. He couldn't imagine his strong, efficient, smart wife crying. There was a core of steel inside of her, he realized now, an integrity nothing could puncture. She had loved the man who'd deserted her for years, remained loyal to him.

Gabriel had never known anyone to be capable of such depth of feeling.

"Please, Papa. Will you be nice to Ellie and ask after her?"

It was the first time his little girl had asked for something. It was the first time she'd looked at him as if he were capable of something good and positive.

But even if she didn't, nothing could stop him from finding out exactly what his wife was crying over. "Of course," he said, hugging his little girl.

CHAPTER EIGHT

It took Gabriel all of two hours to locate his wife.

He looked in the direction in which the groom pointed and came to a standstill at the sight in front of him. With a nod, he dismissed the groom and another staff member, feeling strangely possessive of her.

Without that brisk, matter-of-fact quality to her, she looked fragile and lonely and a rush of protectiveness filled him.

She sat atop a huge pile of hay, her arms around her knees tucked tight against her chest. As if she meant to scrunch herself into nothingness. Shards of sunlight filtered through the wooden slats of the barn, picking out the bronze and gold highlights in her hair. Bathed in the sunlight, she looked like a golden goddess—untouched by cynicism, all soft edges.

"Princesa?"

She looked up, her eyes wide and round in her face. Wariness filled her expression, a sudden tension in the slender set of her shoulders. "Why do you insist on calling me that in that mocking tone? It says you think I'm anything but."

"Does it matter if I think you a princess or not?"

"No," she said, half to herself. "Did you need something? Is Angelina looking for me?"

"I don't need anything, but Angelina's worried for you."

"She's sweet, but I didn't think it was proper for her to see me like this."

"I defer to your superior judgment on that."

"Why are you suddenly being nice to me?" she said, not even looking at him.

"I have been ordered to be nice to you. With the fiercest of threats."

"Ah...now I get it. This is Angelina's doing." As if he did not give a damn about her.

"If I had known you were...unwell, I would have come after you myself."

"Please, all we have is honesty, Gabriel. Don't take that away too."

"Relationships are not my strong point and ours...our relationship hasn't been easy or straightforward from the beginning."

"Because you decided that I deceived you. Because you're incapable of trust."

That kiss had stood between them from the beginning. He had unburdened himself, thinking her a stranger. But what if she'd been telling the truth and all she'd wanted was a simple kiss?

What if the truth was really that simple and that complicated?

Even as she pretended to be happy with her

lot, that version of Eleni had been so vulnerably open.

I wanted to be someone else for one night.

And he'd taken it away from her. "I was angry that day. I had just found out what Monique had hidden from me. I came to the ball wanting to be anyone but myself. Women and deceit seemed to go hand in hand in my head that night.

"I knew the Princess of Drakon. Finding out that the enchantress I had just kissed was that princess was a shock. Like nothing was the same or sane in my life anymore. I don't think I even realized how much I had begun to count on you. How much your presence meant."

"You're just saying that now."

"No. There was always a quiet strength about you, even back then. No wonder you were the only one your father listened to, the only one who could calm his rages."

A strange stillness came over her as he closed the door behind him and drenched them in darkness.

With the world and the day shut away, there was a damp chill in the barn. The setting sun sent tendrils of orange light through the rafters. The long line of her neck bared, she looked up at him, the golden flecks in her eyes becoming prominent in the shadows. He saw her swallow as he reached her, saw that flash of yearning before she blinked and shut it away.

Her arms tightened around her. "I came here to be alone." Even when he'd been his snarliest, grumpiest self, she'd never used that tone on him. Like she had no use for him.

"So that you could grieve over…over *him* in private?"

The same thought would have sent him running in the opposite direction even a week ago. Today, he wanted to comfort her.

Gabriel Marquez comforting his wife over the loss of her lover. Surely the world had turned upside down?

"Yes, something like that."

"You're stuck with me, *Princesa*." The words left his mouth and he realized he meant it. In more ways than one.

He lowered his huge body next to her on the same pile of hay and she instantly shifted. But she was limited by the wall on the other side and his thigh pressed against hers.

The sides of their bodies pressed, and then folded against each other, the soft whisper of it amplified in the dark. The scent of hay and damp earth filled his nostrils.

"Eleni…no one is worth your tears."

"He is. I've known him for years. I've loved him for years. He never looked at me as if I would not measure up. And now I have to say goodbye."

Bitterness mixed with grudging respect filled him. Every atom of his being revolted against having this discussion.

He had the emotional constitution of a car, a lover had once said to him and he'd only laughed and agreed. He'd never been possessive or jealous, for all his relationships had been transient.

Now he couldn't even name the riot of feelings inside of him.

"So you're admitting—" he half choked on the words "—that you're in love with this…man?"

She moved in a blur in front of him, her eyes flashing catlike in the dark. "What? What the hell are you talking about?"

"Angelina told me how much you were grieving over the loss of an old friend. That you had been unbearably sad—"

"Angelina is talking about Black Shadow, my horse of six years."

"Your horse?"

"Yes, my horse, you…you…unfeeling ass. My horse, who I've just found out is terminally ill. My horse who is my closest friend and companion. You actually think I was sitting here crying over some lost lover and that I would tell Angelina about it? What the hell is wrong with you?"

She didn't give him a chance to respond, but

came at him like a flash of lightning—dazzling and beautiful in one breath. Her hands thumped him in soft blows. Gabriel put his hands up, afraid of his petite wife hurting herself rather than him. In his overcompensation, he pushed her off the pile and she took him with her.

He landed on top of her on more hay, his heart lighter than it had been in days.

She hadn't been moping over her lover. He wanted to shout it like a teenage boy who'd found out that the girl he liked liked him back. He felt a lightness he hadn't felt even in his younger, carefree days.

Eleni let out a soft woof as his body pressed her down. "Get off me, you...you unfeeling giant."

He laughed and shifted just enough to ensure he didn't crush her.

She struggled to push him off, as if that were possible, and the slide and shift of her body under his sent his lust into overdrive.

Hell, he liked having her beneath him, all soft and glaring. Another wiggle and her legs separated and straddled him until his hardness nestled against the hottest and softest part of her.

Gabriel let out a filthy oath just as her soft groan filled the air. His hips flexed and rolled in an instinct old as time, his muscles burning with desire. "And if I don't want to move?" He gripped her wrists and pulled them above him, forcing her to look at him. The move forced her upper body to arch toward him, those lush breasts to rub against his chest in the most decadent pleasure. "You have been tormenting me for three weeks, *mia cariña*. Have you any idea what unspent arousal of so many days does to a man?"

It felt as if all the air from the entire world had been ripped out. Leaving only the sensual haze for Eleni to subsist on. Gray eyes watched her as if she were the most delicious dessert that he intended to feast on.

His fingers gripped her wrists in a firm clasp yet gently for a man so big. For days, she had seen him around the suite, in various torturous states of undress, and she knew the power in his muscled frame.

For days and quite a few nights, when he had come to bed and the huge mattress dipped beneath his weight, she had wondered about what it would feel like to be the woman he focused that power on. To be the woman trapped beneath that powerful body.

Shivers had overtaken her at the game she'd been playing every time that gray gaze had swept over her, embers of dark desire in his eyes.

Now she knew.

He didn't quite crush her to the ground but he was a divine, languorous weight on top of her body. Eleni licked her lips, twice, a deep, delicious ache building between her legs. Muscular thighs straddled hers and yet somehow, he kept his lower body away from her, after that first sizzling contact.

Her fingers wound around his upper arms, and she felt the taut clench of his thick muscles. "You're the most aggravating man I've ever met. Tell me, what would you have done if I said yes, Gabriel? If I had truly been moping over my lover?"

He bent his head and the warmth of his breath caressed her trembling lips. She should say no, tell him that she was a real woman with feelings. Not a robot he could use when he needed a mother for his girl, and then ignore.

Holding her gaze, he slanted the angle and pressed his mouth against hers—full flush.

Soft and yet hard, his lips sent a shock that jerked her body into superawareness. Again and again, he did it—moved his lips over hers in a sensual rhythm so visceral that she shivered from the onslaught of it. The world outside the dark barn, the thread of her grief inside, everything fell away under the intense and growing ache within her.

She had waited years, no aeons, it seemed, for the stamp of his body. To be possessed by him.

"I would have reminded you that you promised your body to me, *Princesa*." Only then did he press his hard body into hers. The weight and heat of his erection pressed against her mound and Eleni cried out loud, her body restless in her own skin. Instantly, her thighs created a cradle for him. A satisfied gleam appeared in his gray eyes. "I would have told you that you belonged to me."

Eleni didn't know if she was capable of voicing a question, of asking the same of him, demanding that he promise her the same. He didn't give her the chance to find out. When he finished breathing his guttural promise, he dipped his tongue into her mouth in a long, erotic stroke and Eleni lost the last rational thought in her mind.

"Kiss me back, *Princesa*," he commanded in that same arrogant tone.

Slowly, softly, Eleni opened her mouth and kissed him back.

The raspy slide of their mouths, the heated rush of their breaths, the shiver of hay around them— Eleni had never heard such sensuous sounds in her life. It felt as if every sense of hers was amplified a thousand times over. As if she were nothing but a conduit for sensations.

The strokes of his tongue and lips were maddeningly slow, silky, drawing out the feverish tremors of her body, longer and deeper. The gentleness of his mouth, of his body threw her. It was as if he wanted to savor every stroke of his mouth, hear every gasping hitch of her breath.

As he seduced her mouth with such skill, the barn was drenched in complete darkness. The last fingers of sunlight disappeared and the dark intensified the sensations weaving through her body.

With her hands crawling from his biceps to his shoulders, she dug her fingers into his steel-like shoulders. In answer, he stroked his tongue against hers.

Eleni gasped into his mouth.

She wanted to move; she wanted to touch him everywhere from the torturous prison he created with his own body, but he was so hard and solid over her that she didn't stand a chance. "Gabriel," she whispered, this time it was a plea for more, without doubt.

When he didn't comply, when she could hear the silkily masculine laugh that fell from his mouth, she sank her fingers into his hair and pulled at the thick, rough swaths. Pushed his head toward her with her fingers.

And dug her teeth into his lower lip, driven by an instinct she didn't even know she possessed.

Instantly, he exploded. His kisses became rougher; his tongue plunged deeper and faster into her mouth, imitating the very act of love with such erotic mastery that she was a puddle under him.

The darkness made little of any doubts she would have felt at being naked in front of him when his large hands moved down and, with an economy of movement, undressed her completely.

But when he went to his knees and began pulling his shirt out of his trousers, Eleni wished it weren't so dark in the barn. Her eyes had acclimatized to the shadow and the outline of his body—wide, powerful shoulders, broad chest tapering to narrow hips and the muscular thighs—made her breath go awry.

He was so gorgeously formed—a perfect male and he had chosen her—the short, curvy, diminutive Princess with unruly hair and very little to recommend her.

Was it any wonder the media and the public had such a fascination with their marriage?

When he came back to her and nudged her thighs apart, and then slid his hard body on top of hers, Eleni's head went back in the prickly hay. His skin was like heated velvet, pressing her down.

The rough rasp of hairy thighs against her smooth ones, the press of the hard band of his abdominal muscles against the soft ones in her belly, the silky slide of his chest against her sensitized breasts—a sob flung out of her from the depths of her soul.

Abrasive palms roamed all over her body, learning her curves in the dark. The underside of her arms, the tight dip of her waist, the crease of her thigh—there wasn't an inch of her he didn't worship with his hands. There wasn't an inch of her mouth he didn't devour in long, slow kisses. "Eleni?"

She made some unintelligible sound as his fingers lazily circled her nipple, painfully erect and crying for his attention. Sensations pierced her lower belly, as without any sign, his mouth closed over the hard nub.

A cry that could tear through the rafters rippled out of her as she felt the silky slide of his tongue over her nipple and then the graze of his teeth.

Incomprehensible sounds fell from her mouth as he continued to tease and torment her nipples alternately, as if he couldn't keep his mouth away from them.

A sheen of sweat coated her entire body, her sex damp and swelling. She'd never been so aware of every inch of her body, of every tremor and ripple that shook through her.

"You respond to every touch as if you were an instrument, *Princesa*. You tremble to every touch, you cry in abandon…you have been driving me crazy since that ball."

Her back stiffened when his hand slid down her abdomen. Her cheeks overheated to dangerous levels when his fingers played with the curls there. Masculine demand glittered in every bold stroke, in every invasive touch.

Eleni squeezed her eyes closed, knowing that he watched her. That her pleasure, her moans fueled his own. He took his sweet time, tracing the shape of every fold of her sex intimately, with one finger first and then the next, as if he were memorizing the shape of her down there. As if he had never explored another woman thoroughly before, quite like this.

But of course he had. Every skillful stroke of his, every touch and slide of his lips—he already knew her body better than she did. Better she remember it this time as the most pleasurable, intimate experience of her life, rather than mistake it for emotional closeness.

Rather than delude herself that Gabriel was overtaken by anything other than lust. Afflicted by anything other than a challenge to his pure masculine ego.

Everything she used to convince herself that this was only lust disappeared when he pushed first one and then another finger into her core.

Eleni jerked and locked her hips tight, feeling intensely vulnerable. His fingers were clever as they teased and stroked her, her folds swollen and wet.

"Oh, please," she begged. Was there no part of her he wouldn't discover with intimate knowledge? "Can't you just…I…just want…"

"You just want what, Eleni?"

"I want you inside of me. You don't have to…" His finger hooked inside her wet opening and her eyes rolled back in her head. "Oh, God."

"But I would know your body, *Princesa*. I would

know every gasp and moan of yours, I would learn what would drive you mindless with hunger for me, what would send you over the edge…"

Her hands fisted around locks of hay, her entire body thrumming with a new tension. "You're already doing that," she said on the wave of a sob that filled her when his thumb pressed cleverly against the swollen flesh.

Eleni called out and bucked her hips against his touch, desperate for more.

He stopped immediately and she cursed him to hell and damnation, frustration curling her muscles.

"Do you like this, *Princesa*?" he said, while he dragged his finger in and out, making her wetter and crazier.

Again and again, he tortured her while Eleni lost sight of everything but the deep, visceral want of her body. She forgot the number of times he drove her toward release, and then left her, poised and threatening to shatter, on the edge.

She didn't know when, but at some point, she had given up even on begging him. Just when she had decided he was wreaking revenge on her for wicked reasons of his own, he pushed her legs wider apart.

"That was for all the torment you gave me." His voice was husky, low. "I need you desperately, Eleni. But this is the time to stop me if you don't want this, *Princesa*. After this, you won't belong to anyone but me."

She stared into his eyes and clasped his neck. She could only nod, words failing to come. Or the wrong words. Emotional words that she couldn't sift through for her body was drowning in pleasure.

He slid his hand over her hip, down her boneless thigh and opened her wide for him.

Looking down at her, as if he were one of those conquering marauders that had attacked Drakon again and again, he nudged her opening with the head of his shaft.

Blinking, Eleni fought the furious heat that seemed to combust her from within. Giving up any pretense to modesty, she moaned when he rubbed the full length of himself against her, as if to drench himself in her wetness, and then, just when she thought this torture would never end, he entered her in one deep, soul-wrenching thrust that lodged him inside of her so deep that she didn't know where she ended and he began.

She cried out in shock more than pain, just as the intense pressure inside of her finally combusted and she came in a fierce clenching of her inner muscles.

Hands clenched tightly around his naked back, nails digging into his velvet-rough skin, Eleni tried to make sense of everything that was happening to her.

Her throat felt raw from her cry, her lower belly still clenching and releasing in deep spasms around Gabriel's hard thickness, still getting used to the power and hard heat of him stretching her. Intimate and invasive, being taken by a man with such primitive, possessive need, how was she to keep this in context?

How could she not weave dreams, how could she not tie herself to him forever when he—he did this to her? When it felt like she couldn't breathe again, ever, she couldn't live if he didn't move inside of her? When the thought of him doing all these intimate things with another woman gouged through her very soul?

Pain and pleasure intermingled, her foolish naïveté that she could share his bed, share his life and not lose a part of her splintered, bringing hot, scalding tears to her cheeks.

And in the midst of the emotional and physical storm was the man lying on top of her and staring at her with a thunderstorm in his eyes. "You lied again, *Princesa*."

Eleni bit her lip to puncture the haze around her senses. Her hands roamed over his broad back, traced the deep indent of his spine, as if she couldn't let go of him. A frantic desperation began in her as she realized how deeply Gabriel could hurt her, how enmeshed her life was already with his.

"Stop touching me like that," he said, his voice raised to a storm for the first time against her. The longing in his words resonated in the darkness of the barn, lust etching deep circles around his mouth.

Eleni wriggled under him, trying for succor from the tension in her lower belly, for ease from the continual clenching of her muscles.

"Why didn't you tell me?"

"It was not a question you posed of me when we discussed our marriage. You had very little interest, actually, in anything remotely related to our conjugal life. You barely even kissed me at our wedding."

"You give the impression of a woman who knows her mind, *Princesa*. You said you had been celibate for a long time. You said you loved Spiros."

"You heard what you wanted to hear, Gabriel," she said sounding husky and feeble.

His silence was a deadweight on her chest. "If you're worried that my heart will follow my virginity to you like some kind of bonus offer, please don't. I decided long ago that it would only go to my husband, whoever that was. I couldn't risk the scandal of an affair on top of being illegitimate. Not even for Spiros could I risk the name of the House of Drakos. So my virginity just became another boulder around my neck, another shackle in my fight to be a model daughter for my father."

The bite of his fingers against her hips tightened and she bit back a gasp. Tension thrummed in the hard angles of his face. His skin had a damp sheen, just like hers, and the corded muscles of his neck were so tight that she realized he remained still with a superhuman will.

She sent her hands up his hair-roughened forearms, up his muscled biceps, toward his shoulders. She touched him everywhere and saw the play of tension in his face.

Her heart hammered, waiting for him to push her away, waiting for the explosion she sensed building in him. She didn't know where her boldness came from. But with his hard thickness inside of her, with him poised over her body, Eleni refused to let him go.

She followed the line of his spine down to his buttocks and gripped them. Nudged her body deeper and up toward him.

His snarl sent a spark of sensation down to her pelvis as did the involuntary, instinctual thrust of his narrow hips. "Hold on to me, *Princesa*." He barely gave her time before his hands slid under her body. Rough fingers tilted her bottom up, and then he slid all the way out, and then thrust back in.

Breath hissed through her mouth as he filled her utterly. He did it again and again, in slow, deep thrusts that had Eleni jerking on the hay, heart pumping double time.

The friction he created in that angle was incredible, her body climbing up toward the peak greedily again. Every time he moved, the heat and pressure intensified until her climax burst upon her, in a shower of pleasure and sparks, stealing her very breath.

She was still clutching the white-hot sensation narrowing down in her pelvis, breathing hard when he thrust faster and deeper.

She felt the moment his own tension broke, the moment when he became as irrational as her in his want, felt his spine stiffen. His snarl of pleasure washed over as he climaxed inside of her.

Her hands ached to hold him, but Eleni kept them by her side. That same sense of vulnerability attacked now that the moment was over. Reality came flooding in the form of hard voices approaching the barn, puncturing the magic of the moment.

Pulling out of her, Gabriel dressed with a calm efficiency that made her skin cold. Or was it because the warmth of his body had deserted her?

"Get dressed, *Princesa*," he said, pulling her to her feet and holding her on her jellied legs before she found her balance.

He picked up her clothes and helped her fasten the zipper on her dress. With the soreness between her legs, it took Eleni a few minutes to find her balance. For her heart to stop thumping loudly in her chest.

For her mind to grasp the fact that they hadn't used protection.

She halted Gabriel when he'd have moved away and tried to find his features in the dark. "Gabriel? I..." Heat scoured her cheeks. "I forgot... we forgot. We didn't use protection."

She felt his shock like a tangible entity in the dark. His distress like a stinging slap against her cheek. "Gabriel," she said, reaching out with her fingers, "say something."

The clasp of his fingers around hers sent breath rushing through her lungs. Her legs tangled with his and she fell against his chest. Strong arms wound around her and held her, even as every cell in her braced for rejection. She felt his fingers slide up her nape into her hair, felt the whisper of his breath against her cheek.

It didn't matter that they were standing in pitch dark. She still felt far too vulnerable. One careless word from him could shatter her.

"Then we will welcome the child. This is what you wanted, yes?"

Shaking from head to toe, Eleni nodded. She had been prepared to be overwhelmed by Gabriel's masculinity, but her imagination didn't even come close to reality.

She felt changed from within.

His mouth touched her temple and then drifted down to take her mouth in a long, deep kiss. Bent over his arm, Eleni gave herself up to the languid strokes of his tongue, to the flutterings of desire even through the soreness of her core. A groan rose from the depths of her. Her legs made a space for him voluntarily, inviting him to do more. Waiting with bated breath for more.

His laughter reverberated against her breasts, a silky, confident, utterly male sound. "I would like nothing more than to take you again, *Princesa*, but you would be sore." Something in the tone of his voice set every hair on her body to alert. His grip tightened in her hair, a strange tenseness in his still frame. "Next time you meet a man in some corner of the palace," he said, and she instantly stiffened against him, "or the next time a man drags you into some corner of the palace and kisses you, scream bloody murder. You'll never see Spiros again. Is that clear, Eleni? You'll not even spare him a thought in your head."

Even after everything they had just shared, it was clear he still didn't trust her.

CHAPTER NINE

WITH GABRIEL IN Barcelona for a fortnight's trip and Angelina busy with her tutor, Eleni spent the afternoons with Black Shadow.

She was avoiding facing the reality that was waiting for her in the form of a pregnancy test. Her breath sped up just at the thought, and Black Shadow whinnied, sensing her anxiety.

Keeping her hands on his thick coat, she soothed him with a whisper. If only she could soothe herself so easily too.

She'd longed for a baby of her own for so long yet the possibility of it now left her with panic.

She wanted this baby, of course, with all her heart. A hundred possibilities, happy ones, crowded her every time she thought of holding a baby in her arms. Her and Gabriel's baby. A younger brother or sister for Angelina.

But with their relationship so fragile, so tenuous, she was scared that it would change him, change the way he saw them.

He'd admitted to them being a real family. But she'd no idea if he'd said that in the heat of the moment or if he'd meant it.

After that evening in the barn, he'd walked her

back to her suite and bid her good-night with a lingering kiss. Had told her he had work to catch up on.

When she'd gone to look for him the next morning, he'd already left the palace. Only a text message informed her that he was already en route to the airport heading to Barcelona on company business.

She'd known as surely as the soreness between her legs that morning, the faint fingerprints on her hips from when he'd held her tightly that he was avoiding her.

She'd been glad for the reprieve too. For she'd have never been able to act normal with him the next morning. If her life depended on it, she couldn't have pretended that their encounter in the barn hadn't changed her.

Until she'd learned that at the same time she was mooning over him, Gabriel was in Barcelona with his ever-present lawyer friend, attending parties and generally making merry.

Of course, the media had reported it.

Has the real estate tycoon already lost interest in his new bride?

It was a wake-up call from the fairy tale she'd begun to weave around them. Whether Gabriel had already gone back to his old habits or not,

Eleni needed to face reality. Needed to remember that this was a convenient arrangement.

It was another thing she'd learned about herself.

Making love with Gabriel could never be simple for her. It would mean more, and she'd desperately need for it to mean more to him. For him to never want another woman.

And therein was the problem.

Until she had a handle on her own emotions, she couldn't tell him what she suspected. What she knew to be true in her bones. What she was terrified was in her heart.

Gabriel returned from his trip to Barcelona and went straight to his office to finish signing some documents for his secretary.

Every inch of him was bone tired after dealing with his sister's worries about their mother. Nothing was short of a drama with Isabella. Nothing short of life or death seriousness.

And yet, he was also aware of a mad pulse of excitement inside him. A new awareness of everything around him.

All week, he'd thought of Eleni. Of her crestfallen expression when he'd told her to get dressed in that dismissive tone. Of the way she'd scrunched into herself when he'd warned her that he wanted no lies between them again.

Of the way she'd walked away from him. As

if she couldn't bear to be touched even by his shadow.

Setting up the new rules for their relationship, warning her not to give him a reason to doubt her again—he'd needed to do that to wrest control of the situation. Once she understood his rules for their marriage, she would be fine.

Anticipation tightening every muscle, he walked through the maze-like corridors between the wing that housed his office and the residential apartments at the back of the palace. The famed courtyard glittered with its numerous stones in the moonlight, a cool breeze fluttering in from the ocean.

Never had his heart thumped so hard at the prospect of seeing a woman.

Standing under the hot stream of jets in her bathroom, Eleni breathed deeply, trying to rid the anxiety that seemed to swirl in her belly.

It had started the moment Angelina had smilingly whispered that "Papa had returned" this afternoon.

Every cell in her had wanted to leap across the walls of the palace toward him. Every minute of the day that had passed without seeing him had built up the tension inside of her.

Suddenly, the idea of settling herself in Gabriel's bedroom felt like the most naive, most stupid idea she'd ever had. In retrospect, this whole marriage seemed like one, but she couldn't just back out of it.

She needed a to-do list to take control of her emotions, like everything else. Physical distance first, so that she didn't do something stupid like beg him to trust her.

To want her like she did him.

Keeping her dignity would be bullet point two. That way, he'd not know how much he'd hurt her.

That had been her strategy even with her father. Most days, especially in the end, when his dementia had made him vulnerable to attacks of rage and spite, Eleni would pretend that his barbed words didn't hurt. And for a while, at least, she'd bought into her own pretense.

Wresting control over her body and heart— bullet point three.

The water she'd found soothing until it felt far too hot on her tingling skin. With just the thought of Gabriel and what he'd done to her, she felt far too aware of the crease of her sex, the heaviness of her breasts, the ache that came to life between her legs.

She shut the shower off and tapped her forehead against the cold tile. No bullet points would help the longing in her soul.

Thoughts in a whirlpool, she hastily dressed

in her pajamas, pulled a robe over top and went back to her old bedroom on the opposite side of the wing.

Dawn was tingeing the sky a delicate pink as she flipped the covers over her bed and looked at it restlessly. She was far too keyed up and anxious for sleep. Far too tired to dress for work already.

She was wandering her bedroom restlessly when there was a loud knock on the door to her suite. She opened the door to find Gabriel standing at the threshold, a thunderous expression in his eyes.

Instinctively, she took a step back and his scowl deepened. He saw the night bag she had packed without thought, her laptop case sitting at the foot of the bed. Her cell phone connected to its charger by her bed.

"What the hell is the meaning of this, *Princesa*?"

"Of what?" she forced herself to say, while her mind, and body, became reacquainted with the sheer breadth of his masculinity.

He moved in with a purposeful stride and banged the door closed behind him. Like he'd done at the barn. He wore an expertly tailored white dress shirt that he unbuttoned roughly. All the while his gaze did a thorough, tormenting sweep of her body.

Alarm chased through her with a follow-up of deep want. "I don't need consoling tonight," she blurted out, feeling as if she was turning inside out.

His fingers stilled on his buttons, his head jerking up. "Excuse me?" He strode toward her, and when she backed away, seemed infuriated. "What did you say?"

Eleni licked her lips and wished she'd kept her mouth shut.

He stood so close that she could scent a thread of his aftershave. Her knees threatened to buckle under her.

"Why have you moved back to your own suite, *Princesa*?" Goodness, he was blazingly furious. Again. "Have you already had enough of this marriage?"

Her cheeks burned with mortification. She craned her neck to see into his eyes. "I needed a little distance," she said defensively. "Also, since you left without a word, didn't even bother to ask after me the next morning, I wasn't sure if you wanted me there."

"Wanted you where?"

"In your bed."

Another step of his toward her, and she backed up a little more. "You didn't ask me the first time if I wanted you there. You lodged yourself in my bedroom as if you were queen of the palace."

"I...I was foolish then. I thought if I dangled myself like a juicy carrot in front of you in close quarters, you'd succumb to temptation."

His mouth twitched but nothing could calm the devilish gleam in his eye. He looked at her the way she looked at a pair of stilettos. With deep, possessive need. "And you succeeded. I fell for the proverbial carrot and devoured you." Her blush rose again and she just gave up fighting it. "Is that the problem?" His face softened, tenderness and something else filling up his eyes. "Did I hurt you?"

He looked so utterly pained by the prospect that Eleni couldn't keep quiet. "It hurt, yes, but... not in a bad way. With our respective sizes, Mia said she figured I would be up for a rough ride." This time she burned with mortification for he laughed outright.

It was the most beautiful sound Eleni had ever heard.

"My point is...it hurt no more than it should for my first time. I think."

He pushed a hand through his hair roughly. And slowly, as if coming out of a fog, Eleni wondered if he had truly worried over her absence in the suite. If she'd just declared defeat without even fighting for their marriage. "Then why are you here, Eleni?"

"You left before I... You left without a single

word and you didn't return for a week. Moreover, you stayed with your...lawyer friend, who they say is really close to you. Not everything in this marriage can be your decision, Gabriel. I gave myself whiplash wondering what you were thinking. I wasn't sure if you'd want me in your bed."

"And if I didn't want you, you'd stay out of it, Eleni? Why didn't you do that the first time then?"

This conversation was going nowhere. One of them, Eleni knew, had to take the first step toward the other. Toward honesty in their feelings. In giving more than wanting things in return. In making a leap of faith.

She'd demanded his trust, and yet she hadn't trusted in herself at all. Hadn't believed that she could be his equal, that she could still steer their marriage the way she wanted.

Just like she'd always done with her father. She'd kept her head down, absorbed all his poisonous barbs about her sullied blood, about not being good enough for the House of Drakos with a blind hope that he would come to love her.

God, she'd been such a coward.

But Gabriel meant far more to her than anyone ever had. Then shouldn't she at least fight for him before she gave up?

Hair mussed, shirt hanging open, he'd never looked more gorgeous. Or more out of her reach.

Her chest ached with longing. But she had to say her piece. He undid the last button and, mesmerized by the sight of his tanned, perfect chest, Eleni stared mindlessly. "I thought this would be easy. I would look after Angelina, have a baby and you would never threaten Drakon again. But I realized I just can't. I can't—"

"If you're asking for a bloody divorce two months into this marriage, I will—"

"I'm not!" She stared at him, aghast. "Why do you keep assuming the worst about me?"

He sighed. "Then what do you suggest we do, *cariña*? What is it that you want of me?"

"I realized I need more than you'll ever be willing to give, Gabriel. And I...I can't just let you hurt me. Like I let my father all my life. I'm still trying to find a way around that instead of just giving up on us. But infidelity is my last straw. I know what we agreed, but I just can't..."

The tender stroke of his fingers over her cheek made tears prickle behind her eyes. "I have not touched another woman, nor will I..." Gabriel pushed his hand through his hair, frustration building up inside him. Yet it had nothing on the panic that had swarmed him when he'd found his suite empty of her. She asked for very little. And yet, every word he spoke to her felt like he was giving away parts of himself to her. Permanently.

He still had to try. "I have never slept with two

women at the same time in my life, Eleni. With the relentless media focus on Nikandros and Andreas, you have to know that half of it is smoke."

She lifted her chin and met his gaze, as if to assess if he was speaking the truth. "All I care about right now is Angelina. There are enough headaches in my life dealing with you and Angelina, finishing this project in Drakon and to top it all, my mother is getting married again, apparently, and she thinks somehow I will join her and the new chump she's picked out in this celebration. I went to Barcelona to reassure Isabella that I'll look into it. And if my communication and my departure was abrupt, it is because that's how I have lived for thirty-six years. I won't come to you and discuss every filament of feeling or emotion that passes through my head."

"Feeling?"

"Yes. I felt guilty for taking you like that in the barn. For not listening to you about the video. And I don't handle guilt well. I've never—" He cut himself off right there. "I've never been in a relationship with this much hassle." There! That should satisfy her!

No need for the minx to know how possessive he felt about her. Or about the moments of dread when he wondered about the man she'd loved once, the man who was clearly dear to her. Not when the knowledge of him returning, of him offering Eleni the world hung over him like a shadow every waking moment.

But he would deal with it when it came to that.

She was *his* wife now.

She belonged with him and Angelina.

The sexual chemistry between them was off the charts, and when it cooled, they would both come back to earth. They might even have a satisfactory sex life, a relationship with mutual respect and love for Angelina and any other children they might have.

"You went to see your sister, Isabella?" she asked in a small voice, her gaze searching his.

"Yes. Are there any more questions?"

"Your friend…"

"Alyssa has never been my lover and never will be."

This much emotional seesawing was going to make her go up in flames one of these days, Eleni thought, staring at Gabriel's now completely naked, and utterly sexy, chest.

"Your mother lives in Barcelona?" she somehow managed to also ask.

"Yes. We don't speak to each other so Isabella is kind of the go-between. And now I would really like to end our domestic drama and go to bed."

Eleni nodded, feeling her mouth dry completely. Had they resolved anything? She knew now that he would not cheat on her. But he still had deep trust issues. Issues that he wouldn't talk about easily.

Knees feeling like rubber, she walked toward the bed.

One look at the dark blue sheets sent her scuttling back to the sitting area. Did he want to share the bed with her? Did he expect to make love tonight?

Just the thought of it was enough to send her body into a spiral of longing. Could she make the first move?

She had to be the only woman in the world who could command a palace staff of two hundred and yet worry over her husband coming home to bed at night.

Every beat of her heart seemed to take forever as she heard the shower go on and then off far too soon. In the end, she waited near the window, far too keyed up to sleep.

A towel tied to his waist, his chest still damp from the shower, Gabriel walked out. Any remaining air in her lungs went whoosh.

Dark olive skin stretched over lean muscles. A smattering of dark hair, wetly stuck to his skin now, made a dusky path from his chest to his navel, and then disappeared downward into his towel.

He used another towel to wipe his back, drawing her attention there. Smooth, gleaming skin and broad shoulders... Eleni couldn't stop staring. She only barely remembered to keep breathing.

He plopped onto a chair in front of her and pulled her hands onto his shoulders.

Eleni jerked, the heat of his body singeing her fingertips even through the fabric of his shirt. He was pure steel under her fingers, the span of his shoulders so broad that he encompassed her petite frame. Simply, he took her breath away.

A bird cawed somewhere in the distance. A gentle breeze ruffled in through the French doors. Silence around them thickened until Eleni was sure the thundering of her heart could be heard all around them.

"What...what is it that you expect me to do?"

"I worked for too long in the same pose on the flight. My back aches like hell."

She bristled at the command in his tone. "So?"

Tilting his head to the side, he devoured her with his gaze. "So be a good wife, *Princesa*. Your husband has come home after a long, hard day at work and he needs some attention."

The very devil twinkled in his smile. "Poor Gabriel..."

"This is what marriage is about, you know. Ensuring your husband has everything he needs."

Her mouth twitched, the long-suffering look on his face sending a bubble of laughter up through her throat. "I didn't know you were such an expert on marriage."

He shrugged. "I don't do anything by halves. And *Princesa*?"

Eleni didn't think she'd ever known a moment so filled with utter joy. "What, now?"

"I would have you not work so hard either."

Stunned, she looked down at him. "What?"

"You…are not just the Princess of Drakon anymore, Eleni. You are my wife. You could soak in a diamond-filled tub all day if you wanted. You could give up each and every one of your palace duties. We could…"

"But you accepted my request to stay in Drakon."

"I did. But I still wish for you to make a life outside of the palace. Anything you need, it's yours for the asking, Eleni."

Is your heart available? she wanted to say, but kept the silly question to herself. *One step at a time, Eleni*, she told herself, and right now, all of her energies were consumed by her husband's gloriously naked back.

Pondering his request, she went to work on his muscles. He was right. There were painful knots all over his shoulders and upper back. Even damp, his skin was still warm to her touch.

She kneaded the stiff muscles in silence, working through each knot. Heat flew from her fingers to his skin and back until her own fingers were tingling from it. She didn't know how long she continued like that, but in that small, quiet moment, there was a tenuous connection between them.

The silence went from comfortable to tense, back and forth like the swing of a pendulum. In the next breath, Gabriel turned and lifted her up in his arms.

Eleni could only stare.

He deposited her on the high bed and stood in between her knees. Holding her gaze, he pushed the thin straps of her nightie down, baring her breasts to his slumberous gaze.

"I did you a disservice that night."

"How?"

"In the dark, I could only feel and touch. I couldn't worship you with my eyes."

Rough fingers kneaded and played with the bared flesh, setting her nerves on fire. Her spine arched, her upper body leaning toward him of its own accord, demanding he give her that same spine-tingling pleasure.

With a husky laugh, Gabriel complied. His tongue flicked and played with her nipple, until it was painfully sensitive. Sinking her fingers into his hair, Eleni moaned just as he closed his mouth and suckled deeply.

Sensations flew to the apex of her thighs like molten lava. Her silk nightie slithered soundlessly to the floor. Gabriel pressed a reverent kiss to her soft belly, his breath a harsh rhythm in the silence.

"You're the most beautiful woman I've ever seen, *mi princesa*," he whispered, and looking down at her flushed skin, her trembling muscles, Eleni could well believe it.

How could anything that gave her so much pleasure be anything but?

Pushing her back into the bed, his mouth went on a lazy trail from the valley between her breasts to her abdomen.

Eleni stretched on the bed like a cat, the cool sheets doing nothing to help her overheated skin. When he joined her on the bed and pushed a lazy hair-roughened leg between hers, she moaned at the pressure. He pressed at the spot hungering for his touch with his thick muscle and a soft pulse shuddered there.

"You're already damp for me."

Blushing, she turned to him. Bronzed skin gleaming with vitality, he reminded her again of the marauders that had tried to capture Drakon again and again. She ran her fingers over the spikes of his shoulders, curled them in the crisp smattering of hair on his chest. Heard the hitch of his breath.

She hadn't touched him at all that night. She had only been a receptacle for his mindless caresses. She had waited an entire lifetime for passion like Gabriel had showed her that day, but she'd barely participated.

It had taken her thirty years to take her life into her own hands. It was high time she took the matter of her pleasure into her own hands too. And today, her pleasure was in learning all she could of this hard man who had driven her to the mindless edge that night. Today, she wanted to know what would drive him crazy like he did her.

Today, the Plain Princess of Drakon wanted a little power over her husband.

With a boldness that surprised herself, she pushed him back on to the mattress.

"Eleni?"

She bit her lip, staring at the masculine beauty that was stretched out in front of her. How she wished she'd been a painter like Andreas, so that she could forever memorize the bold, intensely masculine lines of his body. There was such honed strength in him and yet, when he touched her, he was capable of a gentleness she would have never thought possible.

"I want to do this, Gabriel. I want to pleasure you. Will you let me?"

Hands folded behind his head, he raised his brows in a taunt. "I'm all yours, *Princesa.*"

Her eyes darkened, her silky hair falling like a curtain around her face. Candlelight flickered over her lush body, bathing it in a golden glow.

She swept that golden gaze over him thoroughly, from his hair to his toes, lingering over the tent the towel made at his groin.

Gabriel had never met a woman quite like his wife. Determined, even in the darkest of times. Never backing down if she thought it right. Reaching for what she wanted, even when he'd behaved like an ass.

And now she stared at him as if he were a delicious feast. He wanted to push her plush body down and thrust into her, and yet, he had already misused her that way.

Today, he would go slowly if it killed him, and with the way she eyed him it probably would.

"You have to unpack me first, *Princesa*," he taunted, and she blushed again.

Fingers swift and sure, she pulled his towel from under him. Her eyes widened, her breath held as she eyed his erection.

Then slowly, gently, she took him in her hands and squeezed. Her grip was tentative but firm as she studied him with such focus that Gabriel turned into stone in her hands.

"I don't know what to do." She licked her lips with a silky innuendo she wasn't even aware of. "Teach me, please."

His eyes closed, a low growl rumbled out of his mouth. "You're going to be the death of me." He closed his hands on top of hers and showed her how to stroke him. How to drive him out of his own skin.

Sweat broke out on his skin, pleasure balling up in his groin as she pumped him with her hands, just as he showed her.

He felt the silky slide of her hair over his chest, teasing his nipples, turning his abdominal muscles into hard rocks. Her tongue licked the shell of his ear and he bit out the filthiest oath he could think of. "What do you want, Gabriel? All you have to do is tell me."

"Take me in your mouth," he growled without hesitation.

When her heated breath fell on his erection, he opened his eyes. Just in time to see her lush, pink mouth close over the head of him.

Eyes rolling back, Gabriel groaned. His hands plunged into her hair, guiding her to take him deeper. Pleasure built up along his spine. With another oath, Gabriel eased her away.

"Gabriel, wait…"

But he was too far gone now. With one flip of his hand, he pulled her on top of him until she was straddling him. He wanted to feast his eyes on her like this—her breasts with those plump nipples moving, her belly contracting, her spine arching, every inch of her lushness only for his eyes.

"Take me inside you, wife," he said in a voice hardly recognizable as his.

The most beautiful smile flared over her face as he nudged her thighs apart. Tension corkscrewed in his pelvis as she edged the tip of his shaft inside her sheath. Hands on her hips, Gabriel waited for her to get used to him again. Fought the urge to ram upward into her slick warmth.

Slowly, she lowered herself into him, her brow tied in focus, her tongue peeking out to lick at her lips.

Beads of perspiration dotted her upper lip.

Inch by inch, she impaled herself on him in slow torture. When she had sheathed him completely, the tightness was incredible, gloving him like a fist. Slow tremors began in his muscles, desire a knife arching through his spine.

He would have bucked his hips up into her. Except the whimper of discomfort that fell from her mouth stayed him.

Somehow, he leashed his own lust, felt the twitch of his hardness inside of her in protest. Gritting his teeth, he looked at her and his heart thudded against his rib cage.

The stiff arch of her spine reminded him that she was new to this. That her body had been untried until only a week ago.

The slow shift of her hips sent a bolt of pure pleasure through his groin. And yet she was still rigid. He molded her hips in his hands, feeling powerless in the face of her hurt. "Does it hurt, Eleni?"

She opened her eyes, her mouth pinched. "Not hurt, but not quite okay." She wriggled her round bottom and gasped again. "It...it feels like you are everywhere, Gabriel, like you have cleaved me in half. And I'm afraid to move." Sudden tears filled her eyes. "I'm sorry for...I just need a few seconds to get used to you."

"It's okay, *Princesa*. We have all night. We have months to learn each other, years to do all the things I want to do with you."

For some blasted reason that he couldn't fathom, that made tears roll down her cheeks.

She wiped at them roughly. "I wanted to be sexy and alluring with you. Not turn up the waterworks."

Had his trysts with other women been anything like this? At that moment, Gabriel couldn't remember another woman's face, much less any sweet words he'd whispered to one after sex.

Sinking his hands in her hair, he pulled her down, uncaring that he slipped out of her warmth. Uncaring that his body coiled tighter with unspent frustration. "You are the most fascinating woman I've ever met, *Princesa*. And it's not your fault. I...didn't quite prepare you. You're tiny and I'm...a big brute."

She laughed against his mouth. "I can't verify that so I have to take your word for it."

He smacked her bottom playfully and nudged her closer to him. "You will, if I have anything to say for it. Don't worry, *querida*. Once we do get used to each other, I'm going to devour you. You're not going to get out of bed for a week."

Eyes wide like saucers looked up at him. "Yes?"

"Yes. Now shut up and kiss me, wife."

Her breasts were lush and a delicious weight, her belly soft as she nuzzled into him. He took her mouth in a soft kiss, tenderness cutting the hard bite of his lust. Using every bit of his skill, he stroked the recesses of her mouth until she was moaning against him.

Slipping his hands in between them, he touched every inch of her—from her taut nipples to the folds of her sex that were silky wet. Only when she was rubbing against him again, only when he could feel her readiness, did he enter her again.

He kept up the pressure of his fingers, brought her to the peak. The moment she leaned forward and kissed him, he thrust up into her. They groaned, their bodies finding an easy rhythm this time.

As if they knew how to create the magic.

They moved together like some wild things, their mouths kissing and licking, their hands clasped together. When he showed her how to move with him, Eleni followed his instruction, arching her back, trusting her body and his, reveling in Gabriel's hoarse grunts of pleasure, the fact that she had brought this powerful, breathtaking man to such undefinable pleasure.

Pleasure burst on them in tandem, and Eleni fell forward on his broad chest. Curling into him, she closed her eyes. Their bodies were damp, their breaths still labored.

The silence was a blanket over them. Yet every beat of her heart said she had irrevocably fallen in love with her husband. Every pulse in her body, every bead of perspiration on her skin wondered at the hard flesh beneath her. The loud thud of the thundering heart beneath her own—she would know it even in the dark, always.

And with the realization flooded in panic. For she knew Gabriel would never give her his heart. Would never love her as she'd love him whether they were together or not. Whether they had a child or not.

For the rest of her life.

CHAPTER TEN

OVER THE NEXT month Drakon celebrated the fact that their beloved Crown Prince Andreas was back from his mysterious expedition.

It was all Gabriel heard from Eleni, whom he barely saw. She was overjoyed that her older brother was back. The one time he had seen Andreas, Gabriel had gotten quite the shock.

Andreas Drakos had always been a hard man, yet it felt as if there was nothing but a fierce, cold rage in his eyes these days. Now Gabriel had information sitting on his desk that he knew Andreas was looking for, information he had acquired because Eleni had begged him to help her brother.

And he was coming to learn he could not deny his wife anything.

Yet, something in the other man's gaze had held Gabriel's hand back.

The Royal siblings appeared everywhere for a few days, Nikandros leaving his pregnant wife's side with the greatest reluctance. Whispers of a great alliance between the House of Drakos and a cabinet minister's daughter abounded but if there was a man who was less suited to be anyone's husband, it was Andreas Drakos.

The portentous niggle that had beset him from the moment Andreas had returned came true when he was informed that the Crown Prince had requested an audience.

Without Eleni's presence.

Gabriel entered Andreas's office after a short knock.

Any civil greeting he had rehearsed disappeared when he spied not only Nikandros but another man in the room.

Spiros Kanellos, if his sources were right. And they always were. The man his wife had once loved. The man who had disappeared from the face of Drakon for close to a decade. The man who had suddenly reappeared the night of their wedding.

Suddenly, everything fell into place. The man's unhindered access to the palace, his outrageous confidence that Eleni would receive him—he was going to throttle Andreas.

Gabriel refused to acknowledge the man's presence. But of course, he couldn't help noticing the defiance in his expression, the perfect symmetry of his features.

Cold fury filled him and beneath that, for the first time in his life, a sense of doom. "What the hell is the meaning of this, Drakos?" he said, refusing to corral his temper.

Andreas didn't even blink at the menace in Gabriel's tone. "From your expression, I gather you know who Spiros is."

"Yes, since he's been scuttling around the palace and sniffing around my wife's skirts, I had to alert my security force that he was a threat to Eleni and that they could shoot him on sight."

The blond man paled while Nikandros muttered, "Damn it, Marquez."

Andreas held Gabriel's gaze, something moving like shadows in his. "Nik, Spirios, leave us."

Muttering something to himself, Nik escorted the man out.

Gabriel waited maybe two seconds before he gave into the rage building inside him and punched Andreas in his jaw.

The celebrated Crown Prince of Drakos clutched his jaw, nary a curse rising to his mouth.

Gabriel shook his hand, savage satisfaction filling him. "Keep your crooked games to yourself, Drakos. She's not your sister anymore. She's my wife. If you don't want me to sink Drakon, if you ever want to see her again, you will stay out of our lives. I will ruin everything before I let you interfere with us."

Andreas continued as if Gabriel hadn't threatened everything dear to him. "She deserves to be loved, Gabriel. She waited for him for eight years. My damn father lied to her all that time. He intended to tie her to a man of his own age, just so that he could have control over her. So that she would be his willing servant for the rest of her life.

"Spiros loves her. He'll give her what she needs. I know you, better than anyone does. In the end, you'll break her heart. You'll crush her. It's not too late, Gabriel."

"She doesn't need love. She entered this marriage with her eyes open," Gabriel protested, yet there was a hollow ache in his gut. "And what she did want out of it, I can damn well give to my wife."

Even though she was busy during the day with Angelina, and their nights were filled with passion that only seemed to grow the more they fed it, Gabriel knew what Eleni craved. Knew the sudden smile she pulled to her mouth when she saw him.

Knew that his inability to love her would one day pain her. Knew that he was forever waiting for the ax to fall on their relationship. Waiting for something to go wrong.

In every word and smile, there was a part of him that held back. That resisted every attempt Eleni made to get close to him. That measured their marriage still as a successful but convenient arrangement.

Andreas homed in on his hesitation and went for the kill. "All her life, Eleni has been pushed around by my father. By me and even Nikandros. By the stain of her birth. By my father's condescending kindness toward her. By being neither daughter nor staff. I'm fixing all the damage he did to us, Gabe. Nikandros is back where he belongs. Eleni deserves to be given a choice in her life, for once. She needs to have a chance at happiness."

Gabriel had never wanted to throttle a man before. Never had he wished that his heart had remained buried. Never had he wished that he'd never met the Princess of Drakon.

If he gave her the chance, would Eleni choose a life with him? Did it matter to him that she chose it, and was not forced into it?

He set his jaw tight. "I have a file on my desk, Andreas. I have the information you're looking for. And you know why? Because Eleni begged me to help you. Because she worries about you and Nik and all of you."

Every inch of Andreas's face hardened, a dark light coming on in his eyes. Outwardly, he was still. But Gabriel knew the rage that was building up inside him. He would separate Gabriel's limbs with his bare hands, but of course he calmed himself. Nothing remained of his hunger for that information except a gleam in his eyes.

Andreas's self-control was legendary.

"You know where she is?" He couldn't quite hide the quiver in his voice, however.

"Yes," Gabriel replied. "I'll give it to you if you make Spiros disappear. I don't ever want to see him."

Andreas rubbed a shaking hand against his eyes, a small betrayal of his inner state. "I can't. You have no idea how tempted I am to play God. But no more. I will not be like the man who raised me. I will not play with other people's lives."

The hard laugh that fell from Gabriel's mouth was hollow. "And the woman in the file?" Despite his determination to stay out of it, he felt a twinge of pity for her. Andreas Drakos was a determined, cold man, made in the mold of his father, King Theos, however much he fought it. "What do you think you're going to do to her, Andreas?"

"She belongs to me, Gabriel. Keep the information. She could go to the ends of the earth, but I would still find her. My sister, however, deserves a choice. Deserves to choose for once how she wants to spend her life. Either you give it to her or I will."

Studiously avoiding the silent bedroom, Gabriel went into the bathroom, stripped and took a much-needed shower. He dressed himself, wandered into the sitting room and poured himself a drink.

Andreas's words went round and round in his head. The sight of the man she had once loved turned the scotch to ash on his tongue.

Did Andreas actually think he would give up his wife, just like that? Did he think he would let Eleni go to some blond fool who hadn't had the guts to fight for her?

But could he live with Eleni knowing that he had forced this on her? Knowing that all she'd ever wanted of this marriage had been a child? Wouldn't he forever wonder if she'd choose him again given a true choice?

He had no more clarity two hours later when the door opened to the suite and Eleni stood at the threshold. Gabriel had never imagined he'd see a sight that would shred him to powerless pieces as did the sight of his wife's tears.

Pale and drawn out, she stared at him with unseeing eyes.

Tenderness filled Gabriel. "Black Shadow?"

She didn't say anything, only nodded. But even in the dark, he could see the sheen of her eyes.

The depth of her pain unmanned him like nothing could. He never wanted to see it again. He opened his arms and she flew into them like she belonged there. Burrowed into him as though he was her everything.

And for the first time in his life, Gabriel wanted to mean something to a woman.

She was tiny, slender against his hard muscles. And yet, there was strength inside this woman.

Squeezing her against him, he left her not even a little space to avoid him. "Tell me about him," he said, in his usual authoritative tone, realizing only after he had spoken that maybe she needed a gentle hand. But he had never been capable of gentleness.

Maybe she wanted a man who would trust without doubt, who could be romantic without ulterior motives in mind, a man who could give words to the tumult inside him. Maybe she wanted Spiros Kanellos back in her life. The thought was like acid, gouging into him.

"Black Shadow was the only gift, the only thing, really, that my father ever gave me. He cost Father some atrocious amount of money and he refused to let any rider tame him. Father had always been proud of my riding talent, my ease with horses. I was a natural since I was a toddler. It proved to him, I think, that I was truly his—that I belonged to the House of Drakos." She spoke as if the fact was still in doubt. As if she had to justify her presence in the royal household again and again.

Was that why she worked so hard for her brothers? Did Eleni still doubt her place as a daughter of the House of Drakos?

Anger filled Gabriel and his arms tightened around her.

"The moment I saw Black Shadow—his coat gleaming, refusing to trust anyone, but needing a tender touch—I fell in love. I think it was mutual," she said with a smile. "He developed a tumor—" her voice caught "—in his belly, and has been deteriorating for a while now. I went to check on him around dawn. I couldn't sleep at all. It was as if he'd been waiting to say goodbye to me."

He felt the sob build through her small frame. Vining her arms around him, she cried as if her heart was breaking.

Ice that he didn't even know had built in his chest thawed. Gabriel ran his hands over her back, up and down, anxious to soothe her, to assuage her grief. Desperate to give her the world if she needed it.

"Shh, *querida*, he must have known how much you love him."

She wiped her face on his shirt and mumbled an apology into his chest. His heart thundered under those questing fingers. Tonight, his mind was reeling, his emotions whirling.

"Eleni, why did you stay in Drakon all these years? Why not leave? Did you love the mad king so much?"

He felt steel return to her spine and smiled to

himself. "Please don't refer to him like that. His dementia was real and had far too many consequences."

"What about your mother?" He asked the one question that had always bothered him.

"I don't like to talk about her."

He heard the defensiveness that she couldn't quite hide.

He shrugged, keeping his tone casual, as unfamiliar as he was with painful emotions, even he could see that Eleni hid the pain beneath her acceptance of her position in the Royal household. "As Angelina grows up and asks me about her mother, should I lie and keep the memory she has intact? Or should I tell her the truth?"

A long sigh left her and she tentatively laid her head on his shoulder. He knew she understood what he meant. She understood that Angelina already believed, on some level, that her mother had never told Gabriel about her existence.

Painful or not, the little girl had to live with that fact for the rest of her life.

He didn't know why he pushed Eleni, but he wanted her to share it with him. He wanted to know everything about his wife. He wanted to prove to himself that Eleni was better off with him and Angelina. That she had everything she'd ever need.

"My mother was Andreas's nanny. The Queen

apparently had been sick for a long time and she had an affair with Father for years. Things I learned in whispers and rumors from the palace staff. And when she had me, she signed over all rights over me to my father and walked away with a lump of cash. My father might have been controlling, maybe even mad, but he gave me a home. Andreas loved me, in his own way, when he could have hated me for what my mother did to his. Nikandros always told me I was the good one among us. My brothers and my father...they made me feel wanted."

Gabriel searched her face, startled at how innocent she sounded. "How?"

"They needed me. They were always at odds with each other, all three of them, thanks to Father's manipulations. And I was the buffer," she said, as if she hadn't made herself indispensable. As if she hadn't sewn herself into the fabric of their lives.

Did it make her feel useful? Needed? Was that why she'd been so ready to marry him—because she could help with Angelina on one hand and Drakon on the other? The perfect solution for Eleni because her heart already belonged to another?

"In the end, it turned out only I could manage Father. I owe them so much. How could I just walk away? You asked me that night why I wanted to escape who I was.

"Drakon is in my blood as much as it is in Andreas's and Nik's. Even if Andreas found some poor man to marry me—and can you imagine who he would choose?—he wouldn't have understood my attachment to Drakon. He would only marry me as a favor to one of my brothers, or as a business transaction. Even with his cruel taunts, I think my father did a good job of binding me to Drakon, as well as he did my brothers."

"What about love, *Princesa*?"

She looked up at him, her eyes bright with the sheen of tears shed. "What about it?"

"Is it not something every woman wants?"

Lashes flicking down, she hid her expression. "Not me. I…between Spiros and Father and my mother abandoning me, I lost the taste for it, Gabriel." Her voice wavered, a faint tension in her shoulders.

His own breath halted in his throat as Gabriel waited. With every word she said, Andreas's words made more and more sense.

Eleni had never been given the choice to be anything other than what she was, had never had the chance to love herself or anyone else.

"I don't think I even know what love is anymore. If not for Nik's mother and Andreas and

Nikandros, I wouldn't even have known what kindness was."

He should have let it go then. Raking up the past would get them nowhere. He was her present. He was her future. For Angelina's sake, he needed to be selfish.

But then who would put *her* first? Clearly, no one ever had. He was beginning to understand that Andreas and Nik tried to, was beginning to see what had led Andreas to play God from behind the curtain.

So he spoke, his own motives unclear, only the need to see into her soul propelling him ahead. "How could a paid employee like your mother, a woman at that, have had any bargaining power with King Theos when he found out that she was pregnant with his child? The whole world knows of his obsession with his progeny, his obsession with the succession of House Drakos. Legitimate or not, you were still his blood and I bet he gave her no choice."

"I would have never given up on a child of mine, under any kind of pressure," Eleni protested. But there was no conviction in her own words.

"He was a ruthless, cruel bastard, *Princesa*." Remembering what Andreas had said, rage shook his voice. "If he gave you a home, Eleni, he did it to stroke his own ego, to cast himself in a better light. Nothing more."

"So I'll never know what she might have wanted," Eleni said through a throat filled with glass. Gabriel's arms tightened around her while her mind whirled.

The small hurts that had amassed over the years, that she had told herself didn't really matter became a wound Eleni couldn't ignore now.

She knew what kind of a man her father had been. How had she never wondered what her mother's situation had been? How had she never questioned his constant condescension toward her?

I gave you a home when she didn't want you, he would say again and again to her until it was all Eleni had heard growing up.

Until her childish mind had been twisted inside out, until pleasing her impossible father had become her life's goal.

A cold sweat drenched her as she thought of the number of times he had reminded her that she should be grateful to him. That she owed it to him, and then to her brothers.

All the times she had internalized that only by becoming indispensable to her father and her brothers did she deserve a place in the palace.

The time he had flown into a rage because she had said she wanted to marry Spiros. Only Andreas's hand had stayed his rage. Andreas, who had stood between her and what would have been marriage to a man thrice her age.

Andreas had tried, she knew, especially in the past few years. He had, again and again, told her to make a life for herself. Told her that she owed neither him nor Nikandros anything. That she had paid for her father's abusive kindness to her a thousand times over.

But the feeling that she alone would never be enough, that she had to earn a place with her brothers, that she had to prove that she belonged with them couldn't be shaken. She dealt with all her relationships the same way.

Numbness filled her very veins as she saw herself clearly for the first time.

The only reason she'd boldly offered to marry Gabriel had been because she could be a mother to Angelina. Oh, she'd demanded so many things of him and yet hid her own self-worth behind her affection for the little girl. Had told herself it was inevitable if she wanted to save Drakon.

It was the same fear that clamped over her heart every time she wanted to tell Gabriel that they were going to have a child—that stole the words from her mouth when she wanted to demand that he love her like she did him. It was that feeling of not being enough that ran through her when she saw the strides Angelina and Gabriel had made toward each other.

Fear that whispered in her ear that soon, very soon, he would not need her anymore. That there would be nothing of value she would be bringing to their relationship.

She hid her face in his chest and waited for the panic to pass. For the knot in her belly to relent. The scent of Gabriel's skin filled her pores and she never wanted to leave his arms again.

But instead of telling him that, Eleni tilted her head back and said, "Gabriel, will you make love to me?"

She saw the fragment of hesitation in his eyes before he pressed a kiss to her temple. "Princess, there's something we have to talk about."

Eleni straightened in his lap and her hands stole under the opening of his shirt. Warm skin and hard muscles met her palms. The beat of his heart an anchor in her world. His scent sank through her muscles, instantly filling her with a sense of rightness, of goodness.

Gabriel had somehow become the center of her world.

She bent and pressed her mouth to his collarbone. Salt and man—he tasted of heaven. The hitch of his breath, the shift and clench of his muscles, right now, it was all she wanted. Desperately needed. "No, Gabriel," she whispered against his skin. Pulling his shirt open, she trailed her mouth down his chest to his abdomen, until she was on her knees in front of his chair. His thighs were so hard under her hands.

She traced the outline of his erection through his trousers with her knuckles, desire a wild thing inside of her. Looking up, she saw the darkening of those steel-gray eyes, the granite-tight clasp of his jaw, the rigid clamp of his fists against the armrest.

He wanted her. Gabriel Marquez—powerful real estate mogul, gorgeous man, who cloaked his love for his daughter under duty, a man who with harsh words made Eleni see what she could be—this man wanted her.

Slowly she tugged his zipper and began to pull his trousers down.

His fingers on her wrists stayed her, his voice when he spoke, guttural and deep. "*Princesa*, let me love you. You're upset and emotional. You don't have to do this."

Pushing her hair away from her face, Eleni smiled. "No, I don't have to do it, Gabriel. But I want to do it."

In all her life, she had tried to be an exceptional daughter, a good sister, a blameless princess, a friend, a doyenne of charities. All roles she had thought would bring her happiness, would finally earn her a place to belong.

Even when she had married Gabriel, she had done it for Angelina, for Drakon.

But this, this she wanted to do for herself.

The hiss of his breath was a balm to her soul

as she took his erection in hand and stroked it. Warmth pooled between her thighs as she licked the soft top, and then the underside.

Hands sank into her hair, guiding her mouth over his hardness. The taste of him was wild, his groans and filthy curses sending shock pulses to her own core. In this moment, in the darkness of this night, in the privacy of their bedroom, she owned this man.

She continued to lave and lick his length, shivering with her own desire.

Rough hands pulled her away from him. When his mouth met hers, it was like a tempest had swirled into the room. As if he wanted to brand her just as she wanted to brand him. As if he wanted to possess her.

His lips nipped and claimed hers in a mad dance, his tongue dipping in and out in an age-old rhythm. Legs falling away to make a place for him, Eleni cried when his erection rubbed against her belly.

Gabriel wanted her. For now that had to be enough. Later, she would make a plan to keep him. With nothing else to offer him, but just her love. Just herself.

Eleni Drakos Marquez, Princess of Drakon.

"You're mine, *Princesa*," he bit out in such a possessive voice that she drowned in it. He pulled the sleeves of her dress down, filling his hands with her breasts. Pinched the taut nipples until Eleni was arching into his body, a slave to his will. "Say it."

"I'm yours, Gabriel," she whispered against his mouth. And he tasted her in another lingering kiss.

When he pushed her onto the bed and rucked up her dress, when he entered her from behind without that tenderness that had marked all the times they had made love, Eleni exulted in the glorious sensations of being possessed by him. Reveled that she could break his control, bring him to this desperate need.

They moved in perfect rhythm, woman and man, made for this dance, made for each other. When climax burst on them in tandem, Eleni didn't know where she ended and where he began.

When he collapsed on top of her and kissed her temple, she smiled back at him, uncaring of what he saw in her eyes.

Words piled onto her tongue, words she wanted to scream to the world, to him, words she wanted returned. Instead, she poured it all into her kiss.

For now, there was hope and she would grab it with both hands.

CHAPTER ELEVEN

"Ellie, Ellie...where are you?"

Eleni turned away from the mirror, where she'd been examining the faint swell of her belly and pulled down the loose tunic she was wearing.

She had to tell Gabriel soon. But between Andreas returning, the preparations that were in full swing for the coronation, Mia's last weeks of pregnancy and Gabriel traveling more and more, she just hadn't found the right moment.

Or more precisely, she was pooling her courage. And in the process, was overly complicating everything.

Not that the escalating tension between her husband and Andreas helped. Every time Gabriel was back home, and Eleni insisted that they all dine together, a battle of some sort emerged between them.

Neither did it help that she sometimes felt a niggle that Gabriel was slowly pulling away from her. He still laughed with her, teased her about her devotion to all things Drakon, spent his free time with her and Angelina. Made love to her with such possessive passion, drawing it out for so long that she was cursing him, and sometimes with such heartbreaking tenderness that Eleni fell in love with him all over again.

And yet, when they were in bed after he thoroughly exhausted her, when they watched Angelina perform in the local equestrian competition, or when he was away and he called every day to check on Angelina, some sort of tension filled the air.

A distance, an infinitesimal retreat, as if his mind was faraway. Or on something else.

She reminded herself that Gabriel's business consumed his attention, that it was a hard taskmaster. And she was okay with it too, for her hands were full with her own duties. But, still she felt the distance.

Which only made her postpone the truth for a bit longer.

She sighed and turned just as Angelina walked into her bedroom. Her bony arms thrown around Eleni, she hugged her hard. Eleni swallowed and patted her head, her heart full. Soon, she would be holding another baby in her hands.

"You stink of the stables, Angelina," she said with a laugh.

Eyes much like her father's, Angelina smiled back. Her obsession with horses only made Eleni's comment a compliment. "I spoke to Papa this morning. And he's returning this afternoon.

Instantly, her heart raced in her chest. "When?"

"He has a surprise for you. He said I could tell you ahead of time." The girl couldn't stay still for her excitement. "Oh, Ellie, you're going to love it so much." She threw her chest out, her chin lifted. "He asked me for help, you know. So we picked it together."

By now, even Eleni's excitement was boundless. In the last few weeks, Gabriel had been showering her with gifts. Jewelry, couture dresses, a ski lodge in the mountains that they had weekended at once with Angelina, a mansion he was designing himself a few kilometers from the palace—if Eleni ever wanted to leave the palace and live away from her obnoxious brothers, he'd said when she'd laughed and asked what she'd do with a mansion...

The presents were endless, expensive.

"If I didn't know better, I would say you were trying to buy me, Gabriel," she had said with a teasing wink.

But instead of laughing, as he always did when they talked about their relationship, a strange tightness had emerged around his mouth. "Just ensuring that you have everything you could want, *Princesa*."

It had been the perfect moment to tell him that all Eleni could ever want was him. That he'd given her the world and its joys in the form of Angelina and the baby in her womb. That he had given her a sense of herself.

Coward that she was, she had just taken his hand in hers and kissed his palm.

"Ellie, you've got to see it."

"But doesn't he want to give it to me?" she said, playing along with Angelina. Not that she had to fake her excitement.

Angelina laughed, a bubbly, cheerful sound that made Ellie sigh with quiet joy. "This is not something he could give you like that, Ellie. And I bet he won't mind so much if you see it beforehand."

"Okay, fine, you have got me hooked now. Where is it?"

"In the stables. Can I go with you, Ellie, Please?"

Eleni shook her head, knowing how much Angelina was like her father in trying to get her way. "Your math tutor is here, Angelina. How about you and I and your papa can go see it again, once he is back?" When Angelina nodded, she pressed a quick kiss to her cheek. "Please, shower before you see Mr. Stephanapolis," she said, scrunching her nose.

Her heart beat a rapid tattoo as she straightened her hair and pushed her feet into pumps. Angelina would probably have shown more composure in the same situation than her, but somehow she didn't give a damn about propriety right then.

Every time he went away on one of his trips, Eleni felt as if she was losing a limb.

She wanted to ask him to take her and Angelina along. She desperately wanted to tell him that the time he was gone felt like an eternity. She also wanted to tell him that she loved him with all her heart, even when he was his grumpiest and un-communicative as he'd been the past few weeks.

A nervous sort of quiet reined over the stables when she finally got there.

Sounds from Black Shadow's empty stall sent her heart racing. She hurried over and then leaned against the opposite wall, her knees barely holding her up.

The Thoroughbred was tall, at least sixteen hands, and athletic with a dark brown, gleaming coat. A thing of utter beauty and male perfection, like the man who had bought it for her. Proud and arrogant too, just like Gabriel, in the way he reared his head when she took a step toward him.

Eleni just watched, her breath taken away by his male beauty. Her hands itched to trace those sloping shoulders but he would not like her to. At least not yet.

Like his Arabian ancestor, he would be very high-strung. And yet the very prospect of taming him with correct training, of forming a bond with him sent excitement fizzing through her veins.

When he was hers, his loyalty would be absolute. His love would be forever and unconditional. It was the same thing she craved from Gabriel.

She had no idea when Gabriel had decided on this, or when he and Angelina had even slipped away without Eleni knowing. Father and daughter were slowly building a tenuous bridge toward each other.

After a few more minutes of watching him, Eleni turned to walk out of the stables. Excitement fizzed through her at the thought of Gabriel returning. This gift, of all the ones he had showered on her, was so special. It said he knew her; it said he'd wanted to see her happy again, even as he understood that she'd always mourn Black Shadow.

She wanted to thank him personally for such an extraordinary gift. For knowing what would make her laugh again. For simply caring about her.

It was more than she'd expected, more than he had signed on for, she knew.

But the weeks she had spent with him, observing his every interaction with Angelina, learning small things about him, also kindled a flicker of hope.

Contrary to the media's endless stories, she knew now that Gabriel was hardly the love-them-and-leave-them type. She knew that he had a deep core of loyalty toward those he considered his. Despite his initial refusal, he'd agreed to help Andreas in his search for whatever it was he was looking for. Neither of them would tell her what was going on, but she left them to it, used as she was to secrets in the palace and happy to allow Andreas some privacy.

When Monique's mother, Angelina's grandmother, had made a tearful phone call begging to see her granddaughter, Eleni had waited with bated breath. Lies or not, it was clear Monique had loved her daughter. And the thought of Angelina, so much like she'd been at that age, being cut off from another person who loved her, had threatened to slice through Eleni.

To her shock, Gabriel had asked her advice, trusted her to have Angelina's best interests at heart. He'd confessed with a never-before-seen flicker of emotion that every instinct of his wanted to refuse the older woman's request. To cut off his daughter from her mother's family completely.

In the end, he had listened to Eleni's advice that Angelina only benefited from the presence in her life of people who loved her like that.

He'd had Monique's mother chartered to Drakon on his personal jet. However, he had insisted that Eleni accompany Angelina and her grandmother on their day-long tour of Drakon. Had even joined them for dinner that night and had been a charming companion after a satisfactory assessment of Monique's mother.

Her husband, for all his denial of emotions and deep feelings, Eleni realized, felt very deeply when it came to the people he cared about. It was just very rare for anyone to get so close to him as to notice that.

Would he ever consider Eleni one of those? She

had no idea. Would they ever share anything beyond the physical connection and their parenting of Angelina?

She had hardly taken another step when she saw a shadow enter the stables.

Her heart thundered that it might be Gabriel. Tucking away a strand of hair from her temple, she stepped into the main corridor between the stalls when she saw who it was.

"Hello, Eleni *mou*."

Eleni's head jerked up.

Hair shining like raw gold, a glorious smile illuminating his beautifully defined face, Spiros stared at her.

Eleni stiffened, her heart beating a thousand miles an hour. She didn't want Gabriel to discover them here. She didn't want the fragile truce they had built to shatter so soon. Not ever.

Would he even believe that she had not planned this? Would he understand that this was a conversation she needed to have?

She could not untangle her complex feelings for Gabriel without saying goodbye to her past forever. She could not even trust herself again until she learned why Spiros had abandoned her.

"Hello, Spiros."

Her reached her and took her hands in his. A pang of familiarity pierced her heart. His face had been so dear to her once. The blond hair, the slender frame, the straight, patrician nose—it was like seeing a much-missed, dear old friend. She was glad that he was okay. That he hadn't died in some unfortunate accident as she'd sometimes feared.

"Are you not happy to see me, Eleni?"

"I...I don't know what to feel, Spiros. Or what to say. You got me in a lot of trouble for the stunt you pulled at my wedding reception. You disappeared without a word, and then you walk back in like you belong here."

"I'm sorry about that." He clasped her cheeks, his gaze reverent. Something inside Eleni—maybe that naive nineteen-year-old—ached at his touch. Couldn't help but soften when she remembered how he'd been her only salvation on the toughest days.

If only he'd never left. If only they'd married back then... She didn't know what the future would have held for her then, but suddenly Eleni knew, as well as the beat of her own heart, that Spiros was too late.

And not just because Eleni had said her vows to Angelina and Drakon.

"It took me forever to get into the palace, and when I did it was to see you in your wedding dress, looking incredibly lovely. I lost my mind right then. I hope that arrogant Spaniard was not cruel to you."

"Gabriel is never cruel." And she had known

cruelty at the hands of the mad king. For all his claims to ruthlessness, Gabriel ran his empire with a firm but considerate hand. "Spiros, you left years ago. Without word. Without even a goodbye. Do you honestly expect that nothing has changed in all these years? That I have not changed?"

"But you waited for me, didn't you? You didn't look at another man. You didn't marry until just a few months ago. Andreas told me you didn't. Andreas told me you waited for me, you mourned for me…"

Eleni grabbed the wall behind her, a sick feeling clamping her stomach. Anything that involved her older brother, and the warpath he'd been on since their father's dementia had worsened, did not bode well. For any of them. "What does Andreas have to do with any of this?" And even as she asked the question, things clicked. Andreas asking her about Spiros after their father's death, relentless and incessant. Andreas asking her why she hadn't moved on with her life.

"He's the one who encouraged me to come back to you. He asked me if I still loved you and I said yes. But it was already too late. By the time I sold my business in the States and came back, you were already married to him." Torment flickered across his angelic features while Eleni felt like she had stepped onto a land mine.

When and how had Andreas sought Spiros out?

Was this the source of the tension between him and Gabriel?

She could just imagine Gabriel's fury at Andreas's meddling. Familiar fear flew through her veins. She didn't want to lose either of them.

How like Andreas to pull the strings from behind the curtain. She was going to throttle her older brother.

"Say something, Eleni."

"Why did you leave in the first place?" Eleni bit out loudly, frustration coiling through her. "I was so worried about you. I imagined such horrible scenarios. Couldn't you have owned up to my face that we were done? That you never loved me."

"But I did love you, Eleni. Desperately." Spiros's face fell and pity filled Eleni's chest. "It was your father's doing. He said I wasn't good enough for you then. He said I had to grow some balls. When I told him you would run away with me, he threatened my family. You know how much my father and our family depended on the King's goodwill. I let him...convince me to wait. I felt like I had nothing to offer you. He promised that if I made something of myself, he'd consider me again in a few years. But the condition was that I never see you. Never contact you. So I left, Eleni. I traveled the world. I...made something of myself."

Her heart felt like it had received one final

blow. "I waited and waited for you…and when you never came back I gave up on you. Then after a while, your family said that you'd gone to America. That you'd met someone there and forgotten all about me."

"I'm sure he made them say that." He moved back and forth in the confined space, his movements restless, angry. "Your father…he was mad. He never meant for you to marry me," he said, coming to the same conclusion Eleni had. "He never meant for you to leave his side, Eleni. I was such a fool to believe him."

Her knees shook with the magnitude of her father's casual cruelty.

Spiros was right. Gabriel had been right. Her father had meant to keep her with him for the rest of his life. Like an unpaid staff member, a companion, forever reminded that she owed him for everything in her life.

He'd not only ruined her life but he'd ruined Spiros's too. "Why did you come back now, Spiros?" She couldn't even muster anger for him. She felt nothing.

"I heard the news of King Theos's death. And I knew you were still…waiting for me."

Eleni didn't bother to correct him even though resentment grew in her.

"As you very well know, I'm a married woman now." She jerked away from Spiros, resignation filling her. Suddenly, she felt immensely tired. "I don't love you, not anymore."

"But *I* love *you*, Eleni. I would wait another ten years if it meant you would be mine." How could she tell him that it would come to nothing? That he should have stayed and fought her father, that he shouldn't have let his insecurities drive him away.

Tears filling her face, Eleni let Spiros fold her into his embrace. Her chest ached for him and for her, for the future they could have had. If not for the machinations of a sick old man.

For her own sanity's sake, she wished she felt something for Spiros. She would never break her vows but at least her heart would remain safe from Gabriel.

But even as Spiros held her tight, even as the man she had once loved promised his eternal love to her, nothing moved in her.

He was not overtly tall. He was not broad in the shoulder and narrow in the hips. He didn't look at her with compelling gray eyes. He did not call her *Princesa* in a mocking way and yet somehow mean it.

He didn't deny feeling any emotions. He didn't fiercely protect everyone he considered his. He didn't threaten her powerful brothers for their supposed neglect of her or even the entire world for insulting her.

He simply was not Gabriel.

"I have already made my vows, Spiros," she said, wanting to do him a kindness. Wanting to alleviate her own guilt at the love she felt for Gabriel. "I have made promises to a little girl and her father. I...I cannot walk away from those. I will not break my word. I'm so sorry. There's no future for you and me. Maybe there never was."

Spiros frowned. His hands digging into her shoulders, he said, "This is not over, Eleni *mou*. I refuse to give you up so easily after all these years. The Spaniard does not love you. He cannot make you happy."

Eleni didn't know how long she stayed in the stall after Spiros left, his dire warnings ringing in her ears.

But it didn't matter.

Gabriel had spoiled her for anyone else.

I will not walk away from the promises I made. I will not break my word.

Eleni's words to that man haunted Gabriel throughout the day. Damn it, of all the times for him to walk into the stables, of all the things he had to overhear coming from her mouth.

Had he thought her like his mother once? Or like Monique or his sister, Isabella, fickle and full of deceit?

Now he wished she *was* like them. That she didn't care for anyone except her own happiness.

But of course not.

His wife was a bloody saint, forever willing to sacrifice her own happiness on the altars of others' lives.

It was her choice to give up her happiness, something said in his head. A voice that sounded very much like the ruthless, arrogant man he'd been when he'd threatened to sink Drakon if a mere woman didn't cater to his wishes.

He wanted to, God, how he wanted to forget what he had seen in the damn stables.

The pain of a lost future in her eyes, the tears that had fallen when Spiros had told her what her father had done. The way she had folded into that man's arms as if she had no will left.

He would have given anything to un-see it, to carry on like he had been for weeks now. Putting Andreas off, making plans to take Eleni and Angelina away from the cursed palace, reminding himself again and again that Eleni had chosen this marriage, chosen this over some fantastic notion of love.

That she gave everything to it because she wanted to.

Yet the shadow of the man had hung over them. The idea of him waiting forever and Gabriel hiding it from her, crept into all the small spaces between them, until it had become an invisible wall. Until the guilt of it had made him withdraw from her.

Neither had it been missed by her. More than once, Gabriel had seen her hesitate before she said something to him, had seen the stricken look in her eyes when he didn't meet her gaze or avoided spending time with her.

For weeks, he'd existed in a strange limbo, unwilling to let go of her but unable to live with the gift of her choice.

And now—now that he had seen her face, now that he'd heard what she said, he found it unbearable to live like this any longer.

Was this how his father had felt after his mother had come back? Knowing that she still mourned the lover that had abandoned her, yet unable to turn her away? Gabriel had considered it his weakness.

Had his father loved his mother that much then?

Was this how it felt to love someone?

Because he did. Because he wanted Eleni's happiness above all else. He couldn't bear the thought of the future without her but neither could he live with her, knowing that her heart would forever belong to another. Knowing that he had selfishly stolen her happiness from her.

"Gabriel? When did you return?"

He turned to see Eleni walk toward him in the

sitting room, a shaky smile on her face. Her eyes looked dull, bruised, the remnants of her tears still on them.

"Just an hour ago. I had to sign some documents for my assistant."

She reached him, and then registering his tense pose, a wariness filled her eyes. "I...I've been waiting to see you."

"Why?" he asked abruptly, his heart crawling into her throat.

She took his hands into hers, turned them over and kissed the knuckles. "I...I wanted to thank you for my gift." When he frowned, she sighed. "The Thoroughbred? Angelina spilled the beans, and he and I have already become friends. I'm already a little in love with him." She rose up on her toes and kissed his lips. Only he shifted in the last moment and her lips landed on his jaw.

He nodded, then cleared his throat. But for the life of him, he didn't know what to say to her. It was unbearable to be her husband, to steal the intimacy she gave so willingly when in truth she might wish it on another man.

He hated this power she had over him, hated how weak she made him. How she made him want to put his happiness in her hands, how she made the future without her look like an unending abyss.

A nervous laugh fell from her mouth, pulling

her attention to him. "Gabriel, is everything all right?"

"Eleni…did you see Spiros again?"

Eleni blinked. "I… Gabriel…"

"Just answer the question, *Princesa*."

The harsh note in his tone made her flinch. But she nodded, dread curling up in her chest. This morning, she'd been planning to pour her heart out to him. Now she was afraid to look into his eyes. Afraid that all she would see were distance and indifference.

"Yes, I did. Just an hour ago, in fact. He… Gabriel, it was a conversation he and I needed to have. I needed to see him one last time." Anger flooded her, a much better emotion than the fear stealing up her throat. "You can't believe that I'm having some supersecret affair with him right under your nose. If you think that, you're a—"

"No, I believe you, *Princesa*. What I want to know is if he told you. What your father had done."

"Yes, he did." Tears filled her eyes again. But she didn't grieve over herself. She felt sad for her father, who had only sought to control and manipulate his children and not love them. She felt sad for Spiros, who was a good man, and who had become a pawn in that game. "But you already made me tough, Gabriel. You already opened my eyes to what he'd been."

"So that's it? You're over him now?"

"It's all in the past, Gabriel. I vowed to be your wife, a mother to Angelina. And I've never broken my promise to anyone. Not to my father, not to Spiros, not to Andreas, and I'll definitely not do that to you or Angelina. For better or worse."

Gabriel had never wanted to hear those damn words out of her mouth ever again. It felt as if he couldn't breathe, as if a part of him was being wrenched away. Like there was already a hole in his chest.

He could not do it anymore. He couldn't live with her knowing that she wanted another man, another future. "There's nothing more in this marriage for either of us, is there?"

"What? What are you talking about?"

"Angelina and I understand each other. But still, I would ask that you not terminate our marriage too soon. I'll leave Drakon within the next day. Angelina will stay here with you."

If she had shown a hint of pain, Gabriel would have taken her in his arms. Would have kept her chained to his side. But his wife's mask was back in place. Only the paleness of her face said he'd just ended their marriage.

Eleni had been taught again and again to place someone else's needs above her own. To keep her word, no matter what.

It would take time but she would see why he

had to do this. Why he was ripping out his own heart.

"Why are you doing this?" She ran a hand over her tummy, as if to protect herself. "Gabriel, I don't even understand what you're doing."

"I'm freeing you, *Princesa*, letting you go." He took her face in his hands, unable to resist touching her. "I should never have threatened you in the first place. Never agreed to your counterproposal. You have given me and Angelina enough of your life.

"You're free to pursue whatever, whoever you want. Whatever future you like."

"If this is Andreas's doing, I swear I will rip him apart with my bare hands. Don't do this, Gabriel. This is not right."

"It is right, *Princesa*. The only right thing. The longer we continue this farce, the more I will end up hurting you. How you will convey this to Angelina and not hurt her, I will leave in your capable hands. You see, *Princesa*, I trust you completely. I trust you more than I ever have anyone in my life."

He didn't wait to see what she'd say. He walked out of the Princess of Drakon's life, before she took everything he had.

CHAPTER TWELVE

THE WEEKS FOLLOWING Gabriel's departure were the worst of Eleni's life. Even the cruelest days spent with her father, listening to him rage, struggling to calm him until her arms ached—they were still better than the desolation Gabriel left in his wake.

To the outward world, and thankfully for Angelina, nothing had changed. Somehow, Eleni had convinced the little girl that her father had urgent business that would take months, while leaving the window open for her that she could visit him whenever she wanted.

While Angelina hadn't been completely fooled, she'd decided to play along, for now.

Eleni apparently didn't have the same composure the little girl did. She had confronted Andreas, argued with him, called him names for playing God with her life, sobbed all over him, which had then resulted in a huge row between Nik and Andreas.

It had taken a hugely pregnant Mia to calm her brothers down. And at the end of it, Eleni didn't feel even a little better.

Just that same sense of missing a vital piece of herself.

She was six weeks along now, and hiding it

with baggy tunics, she still hadn't told a soul. It was his right to know first and however furious he had made her, she still couldn't take that away from Gabriel.

He called every night to talk to Angelina while Eleni sat there, pathetically waiting for him to ask for her, pretending to Angelina that she'd already spoken to him. When Spiros had tried to comfort her, she had asked him to leave.

She'd already messed up his life, thanks to her father.

Every cell in her wanted to tell Gabriel about the baby. She knew without a doubt that if anything could bring him back to her, it would be the news of her pregnancy. If he found out that he was going to be a father again, he would bind her to him.

But she didn't want him like that. She didn't want his pity, and neither did she want his duty. She didn't want to be a wife to him if he didn't love her.

Not even for him could she live like that again.

Gabriel walked out onto the acreage behind the stables, looking for his wife.

Stunned, he came to a standstill.

Eleni was riding the huge Thoroughbred, the same beast he had bought for her, astride, through a path cordoned off from the viewing point where he stood. It had been only a few weeks since he had given the horse to her.

Had she already tamed him?

Gabriel's heart jumped into his throat as he saw her urge the horse toward an obstacle course that did not look remotely easy.

His heart stayed in his throat as she jumped each obstacle as if it were a child's game. Not once did she lose her seating on the huge beast. Not once did she lose the focus or the mastery with which she ruled him.

It was almost as if the Thoroughbred and she were soul mates, so easily did the proud beast respond to her. She crouched low over him, whispering commands. Gabriel's pulse sped up dangerously as she crouched low and took the final obstacle with a flourish he had only seen in professional jumpers.

The jumping circuit was clearly a piece of cake for her.

Slowly his heartbeat returned to normal and Gabriel wondered again if he would ever stop being surprised by her. Ever stop wanting her with that soul-wrenching intensity.

Waiting to see what she would do had been torture. After his daughter had told him *Ellie's old friend had left forever*—his daughter had the makings of a spy—waiting in Barcelona to finish dealing with his mother and the aftermath of twenty years of estrangement had been torment.

He waited on the other side of the fence as she jumped off the horse, and then whispered near its ear for long, lingering minutes. If he hadn't seen her take that obstacle course, he wouldn't have believed it now.

The beast seemed huge next to her. She looked fragile, almost breakable, just as she had been in his arms.

He followed a few steps behind her as she led the horse to his stall.

She still hadn't noticed him; she was so immersed in the simple task of grooming the beast. She dismissed the groom, and then filled a trough with oats and water.

Leaning against the opposite stall, Gabriel closed his eyes and let her words, soothing and full of praise, wash over him as she talked to the beast.

Just as she did with Angelina, she took tender care of him. Nothing was beneath her. Nothing was to be hurried.

Her very joy in the simple task suffused the air around them.

She spent almost a half hour brushing the stallion's gleaming coat, all the while telling him what a good boy he was.

The stallion neighed and nuzzled into her face,

and again, the same longing rose up inside of Gabriel.

She had reduced him to feeling jealous of a mute animal?

Her amused laughter filled the barn, flew inside the empty place inside of him he'd never known existed. Something settled there and he refused to question or examine it.

When she stepped out of the stall, he moved out of the shadows and in front of her. Her hair had half flown out of her tight braid, just like Angelina's. Exertion made her skin glow like burnt bronze. Tendrils of flyaway hair stuck to her forehead, coated in sweat.

Her pulse hammering violently at her throat was the only sign that she was affected by his presence. She wore a white shirt and jodhpurs.

The tight pants lovingly delineated the womanly flare of her hips. A bead of sweat ran down her neck as he watched, and disappeared into the lush pillow of her breasts.

Her moans from the long nights they had spent loving each other filled his ears. She had been a revelation in bed, just as she'd been everywhere, willing and wanton in his arms as he taught her new pleasure after new pleasure.

Yet, he'd been the one who was always left breathless, their lovemaking going beyond the physical.

The temptation of her lush body, the scent of her arousal, kicked lust into full gear inside of him. He took a deep breath, trying to corral it now. He never wanted to hurt this woman, through words or actions, he realized.

He needed her warmth, her generous heart, her twisted reasoning, her practical efficiency.

"Hello, *Princesa*."

She lifted her chin in a show of defiance but he had seen the hint of pain in her eyes. Her gaze raked over him with calculated feminine interest that made his body heat up, yet left his heart cold.

"Have you come back to proposition a new arrangement, Gabriel? Because you were right. There's nothing you can offer me anymore." Something about the way she said that sent a coldness unfurling in his gut. "Have you come back only after your little spy told you that I sent Spiros away, that you would not risk anything if you came back now?" He felt the loss of the warmth of her eyes like an ache in his body.

"I wanted you to make a choice, *Princesa*."

"No, you made the choice for me, yet again." Her arms went around herself, her very posture screaming rejection. "Like all the arrogant bastards littered throughout my life. You were no better than my father or Andreas, Gabriel."

He flinched, her words landing like poisonous barbs. "Leaving you was the hardest thing I have ever done."

Tears filled her eyes. "No, Gabriel. Fighting for me, as I have been doing for you all this time, would have been the hardest thing. Putting yourself out there, making yourself vulnerable to me, trusting me with your heart would have been the hardest thing. Christos, you didn't even give me a chance! You just gave up on us as soon as you had no use for me."

How had he not seen how much he was hurting her? Was she right?

Had he hidden his own fear, his own vulnerabilities and called it doing the right thing? Had any woman understood him better than she? "You're right. I…I spent my whole life making myself tough. Not trusting anyone. When I saw you with Spiros, when I heard that I was only a vow to you, I just couldn't bear it. It was as if my worst nightmare had come true."

She scoffed, wiping at the tears on her cheeks roughly. Much like his daughter did when he hurt her with his insensitivity.

"Your word, your loyalty was not enough anymore, *Princesa*."

"What do you mean? What is there that you need that I haven't given you, Gabriel? How have I fallen short, yet again?"

"Your heart," he said, reaching for her, lay-ing his hand on her chest. Her heart thundered under his touch, filling him with such awe that he couldn't speak for several minutes.

She eyed him warily, doubt in her eyes. "Gabriel?"

"I wanted your heart, Eleni. Your generous, kind, loving heart. I didn't want you to be my wife because you made a promise. Or because Angelina needed you. Or because you were programmed to do anything for this damned country. Or worst of all, because we were your only chance at a family of your own. I wanted you to be my wife because your heart belonged to me. Because you belonged with me. Because you couldn't go another day without loving me, just as I couldn't without you."

"Oh, Gabriel," she whispered in such a broken voice that his heart kicked against his chest. Furious tears filled her eyes and sent fear spiraling down his spine.

"Princesa?" he said in such a gentle voice that her tears fell faster. "I cannot give you eight years of your life back. I can't give you back a life with that man. But I would love you with all my heart. I would treasure you every day of our lives. I would give you a brood of children, as many as you want. And I would try to be the best damn husband and father the world has ever seen."

He went on his knees and buried his face in

her soft belly. "Give me a chance, Eleni, and you will never regret it."

Eleni sank to her knees and threw herself into his arms. His embrace felt like heaven, the scent of him coiling tight around her like a safe blanket.

He was hers. Her home. Her place of belonging in the world. He was her everything. Didn't the arrogant, thickheaded man not know that?

"I do love you, Gabriel. You saw me more than anyone else in my life has. You made me feel like I mattered even when you grumbled about it. How you could think Spiros meant anything to me after everything we've been together? Why didn't you just talk to me? Why did you leave like that?"

"I had some things to set right. I...I wanted to be a different man for you in the chance that you chose me. Things that were long due."

"What?"

He settled down onto the grass and pulled her into his lap. She felt the shuddering breath he took, burying his face in her hair. His arms were like clamps around her midriff.

Content and delirious with joy, Eleni waited. This man, this husband of hers was worth waiting for.

"My mother was barely eighteen when her father arranged her marriage to my father, against her every protest. Apparently, he was double her age at thirty-seven, much as he had fallen in love with her.

"Within a year, I was born. And she…I think the marriage killed her dreams. She resented her father, then my father. Then me.

"All through my childhood, she…she went off to clubs and parties, made friends with strange men while my father basically waited for her at home. God, I used to think him such a fool. He gave her everything she'd ask for—dresses, expensive jewelry, the latest car.

"I don't know when she started, but she always took me with her to these parties and clubs. Maybe she felt guilty or maybe she used me as a front with my father. But all I remember growing up is lies on top of lies that she told him. I didn't really care back then because she took me with her everywhere.

"This dazzling, beautiful creature, whom everyone loved, who became the light of every party she went to, she was my mother.

"I trusted her, adored her, would have probably killed my own father if she'd asked me to do it. But then she met this new guy. Until that, I think she was only skating the lines, seeing how far she could go without betraying her vows.

"But this painter came along and she fell for him. I instantly knew she was changing. I begged her not to see him. She promised me she would never leave me behind, that I was 'her little big man,' the love of her life. Only, one night, under the cover of darkness, she left with him."

Her arms went around him and despite the heaviness he felt in his chest every time he talked about his parents, he smiled. He had meant to console her and she had disarmed him yet again.

"In the end, she stayed away for five years. When she came crawling back to him, she was pregnant with my sister."

"Isabella?"

"Yes."

"What did your father do?"

"Against my every argument, he took her back. I despised her for a long time...for putting him through such heartache. To the end, he never looked at another woman, never stopped loving her. She said she was sorry for what she'd done but by then the harm was done. He died a few months later."

"Is that why you...you don't trust women?"

He laughed and she just held on to him. Nothing could ever take away the hollow he felt when he thought of his father, the powerlessness as Gabriel had watched him waste away in the bottle, but how had he thought Eleni would do anything like that?

How had he worried about giving himself over to her?

She was the most generous, most loyal woman he had ever met.

"It's not that I don't trust women, *querida*. I just did not want a committed relationship with one. I promised myself I would never be in his position. Never love so much that even your sense of self-preservation is gone."

"And loving Angelina?"

"Having Angelina has made me rethink everything. On one hand, I can't believe how my mother ever walked out on me. The guilt I think is etched onto her face now.

"On the other, knowing that Angelina will be a woman one day, the idea of her stuck in a marriage to a man double her age…it gives me new perspective.

"For years, my mother wanted to see me. When I heard what your father had done to you…it tore me up. Your pain tore me up.

"And it made me realize what she must have felt. Barely a woman, and saddled with a husband double her age and a son. Caught with no escape or outlet.

"It made me think of how it would have crushed your spirit in a situation like that. I could forgive Andreas anything in the world for stopping your father from doing that to you. When I thought of you, what I had to do became simple, easy."

"What was that?"

"After all these years, I went to see her."

"Oh, Gabriel," Eleni whispered into his neck, love filling her chest. "I wish you had told me this before. I wish I could have been there for you."

"But you were, *Princesa*. You were in my heart. Or else I'd never have understood her pain."

"Was she happy to see you?"

He smiled and there was a depth of joy in it. "She was. She is marrying some guy and I think she thought I wouldn't forgive her for that."

"Are you angry with her again?" Eleni asked, heart aching for him. Because, now she knew, it would only be because he cared. Because he wasn't quite the ruthless man he thought himself to be.

"No. I'm not. I wanted to know more about the guy but I felt it wasn't my place." A hint of his pain, even resentment, maybe, peeked through in his voice. But what he had done was a huge step. Those scars, Eleni knew very well, would take time to heal. "Once I saw her, I couldn't stay away anymore. I couldn't not...see you, *Princesa*.

"Angelina told me you sent Spiros away and I breathed fully for the first time in weeks." He turned toward her and cupped her face. "I love you, *Princesa*. Without fear or reservations. I love you so much that I cannot live without you for a minute."

Heart bursting with happiness, she pressed her

mouth to his and sank into his toe-curling kiss. His mouth drifted from her mouth to her nose, to her temple, to her hair, his arms almost crushing the breath from her lungs. In a deft movement, he pulled her up, a sudden urgency to his movements. "Eleni, I know what I promised, but I have a demand to make of our marriage this time."

Laughing, she went on her toes and pressed her mouth to the pulse at his neck. The powerful man shuddered all around her. "Anything, Gabriel."

"I want us to leave the palace, make a home somewhere else. Anywhere in this world that you want to live in. But not here."

Eleni swallowed away the confusion within. "Because of what Andreas did?"

"Because this palace has sad memories for you. It makes you feel as if you were less than the magnificent woman you are, *Princesa*. I would have you happy, Eleni. You and me and Angelina and all the children we will have."

Eleni laughed at that, joy overflowing in her chest. "That was before I met you, Gabriel. Before I...before you showed me what and who I was. Before you challenged all my preconceived notions about myself. But I can't go, Gabriel. Please, not now."

"Why not, *Princesa*?" he said, clasping her cheeks with a tenderness that always snagged her heart.

"I wish I could hate Andreas for his interference, Gabriel. It was just like my father, though I didn't have the heart to tell him that. In those moments when I thought you would never return, when I lay in our bed alone, longing for you… I did hate him then. But he means well. He did it out of love for me. You know that, don't you? He did the right thing, in his own twisted way."

Gabriel nodded.

Only Gabriel's love for Eleni, his respect for everything Nikandros had accomplished in the past year had stopped him from making hell rain on Andreas and his precious Drakon for his interference. Something had happened to Andreas and he felt pity for the woman he was searching for when he found her.

"Andreas made me see I had no choice. Not if I loved you. I hated that he was right, but I had to do it. I had to walk away. But I do not like you anywhere near his controlling influence, *Tesoro*. I do not like him playing with us as if we were pawns."

Tears filled her eyes. "All my life, I've been the buffer between him and Father, him and Nik, Nik and Father. I couldn't take it if you asked me to not see him. If you made me choose between you, I would choose you, yes. But please don't make me.

"He…something's wrong with him. He's possessed, Gabriel. He needs me. He needs us."

Gabriel shook his head, amazed at the generosity of his wife yet again. At her capacity to forgive and forget, at her capacity to love. He took her in his arms again, the sight of her tears unmanning him. In her eyes, in the love she evoked in her hard-hearted brother, Gabriel saw even a chance for Andreas. A slim one. "Andreas doesn't need us, *Princesa*. But yes, until he finds what he does need, we will stay. We will watch over your brother, but not a single day after that."

He kissed her eyes, letting the rush of love and fear flood him. Understanding that loving this fierce woman meant accepting that there would be others who could hurt her. Accepting that she loved everyone without reservations. He pulled her to him and held her tightly. "I will not share you with anyone ever again, *Princesa*. Not with Nikandros, not with Andreas and not with Drakon, yes?"

"You might have to, Gabriel," Eleni whispered against his lips, her heart bursting with happiness.

"What?" he said, scowling.

Eleni pushed a thick lock of hair away from his strong face, her breath stuttering in her throat. She pulled his hand down to her belly and smiled at him.

His gaze flitted up to her face and back down

a few times, before it became wary, almost blank. "When would you have told me?" It was a whisper but she heard his growl in it anyway.

"When you decided that you loved me, Gabriel." She clasped his cheeks and forced him to look at her. "If I had told you, you would have taken over my life. You would have made me your wife whether or not—"

"My child and my wife belong with me."

"Whether or not, you loved me? Can't you see? I couldn't take the chance. I couldn't live like that again. I love you, Gabriel. And I will never hide anything from you ever."

Slowly, the anger abated and he kissed her gently. "You better keep that promise, *Princesa*, or you will learn what a grumpy beast I can be."

Eleni laughed. Grumpy beast or not, he was the man who loved her.

EPILOGUE

Maria Drakos Marquez, a tiny bundle that fit in her father's hands, arrived seven months later with a boisterous cry that declared she was no sweet angel.

With thick black hair and gray eyes, she stared out at her father, her cherubic mouth scrunched tight in protest.

His heart had crawled into his throat a few hours ago when his wife's pains had started. Now, as she looked at his baby infant, it seemed as if his heart would never return to his chest.

That life would never cease to amaze him.

And it was all due to his wife.

Gabriel looked at Eleni, an overwhelming tightness in his throat. Each day he spent with his wife and daughter, each moment of joy that touched their lives, he thought couldn't beat another.

And yet, his life seemed to be filled with such glorious moments. With such all-encompassing joy.

"Let me see, Papa," Angelina cooed in his ear, tugging nervously at his arm.

"Slowly, *pequeña*," he whispered, glad to see that his oldest showed no evidence of feeling left out or neglected. Of course, he didn't know who had been more excited about the little girl's arrival—him or Angelina.

Angelina's eyes widened with awe as she traced her little sister's tiny hands in a reverent touch. "She's so tiny, Papa. I…"

He understood exactly how Angelina felt.

He felt both happiness and trepidation that the care and well-being of someone so fragile was in his hands now.

Gabriel carefully handed his precious little baby to his own mother, whose eyes were overflowing with tears. Angelina instantly drifted off toward the baby but before she did, she threw her arms around Eleni, pressed a fierce kiss to her forehead and whispered "I love you, Ellie."

Gabriel smiled as his brothers-in-law, Andreas and Nikandros, crowded around his mama, waiting for their turn to look at his new daughter. His heart thudded in his chest as Andreas took her in his arms and cooed at her. His tone and the slight tremble of his hands belied the fiercely unemotional expression on his face. The hollows of his face became even more pinched as he studied his tiny niece.

Gabriel looked away and took a deep breath.

From Andreas, Maria went to Nik, who carried her with the aplomb and finesse of a new father.

There were so many people who would love Maria. So many who would nurture her and ensure that she was taken care of. And if he made a misstep, his wife would correct him, show him how to love this tiny being.

His lungs expelled in a sudden rush.

"Gabriel?"

The husky, raw tones of his wife made him look up. Sweat pasted thick tendrils of her hair to Eleni's forehead, her eyes sleep-deprived, yet to Gabriel, she had never looked more beautiful.

"Yes, *Princesa*?"

She extended her hand and he took it. Lifting it to his mouth, he pressed a tender kiss to the inside of her wrist. She clasped his jaw, as if she understood the enormity of his emotional reaction to their little daughter.

The wetness behind his eyes slowly abated. To his wife's raised brows, he somehow managed to squeeze himself into the tiny bed and wrapped his arm around her. The others had left the room.

"Was that your mother, Gabriel?"

Nothing went missed by his superefficient wife. "Hmm."

"You asked her to visit?"

"Yes. I…" He nuzzled into her neck, needing the warmth and scent of her. "When you went into labor, I couldn't bear it. I called her and she offered to jump on a plane within minutes. So I sent her my jet and she got here a few minutes before Maria arrived. You've brought me so much love, Eleni, that it seems very hard to hold on to the past, to hold on to anger. There's no place in my heart, it seems, for anything more than love."

"I understand, Gabriel. Loving you has taught me to love myself."

He pushed off a lock of her hair and pressed a kiss to her temple. "*Te amo, Princesa.* With all my heart."

She took his hand and kissed it, her eyelids droopy, her mouth trembling. "Thank you for loving me, Gabriel. Thank you for giving me two wonderful daughters."

"Thank you for making a family with me, *Princesa*," he said.

Within minutes, she was out like a light. When his mother returned a little later and handed him Maria, Gabriel said everything he had to in a kiss on his mother's cheek.

And went back to the bed, sleepy bundle in hand, to wait for his wife to wake up and kiss him again.

Looking at the tight fist that formed around his finger, he realized he was in for a long wait and sighed.

But he didn't care.

The Princess of Drakon and her kisses were worth waiting for.

* * * * *

If you enjoyed
THE DRAKON BABY BARGAIN,
why not read the first installment of
Tara Pammi's
THE DRAKON ROYALS *trilogy?*
CROWNED FOR THE DRAKON LEGACY
Available now!

And look out for Andreas's story,
coming September 2017

Get 2 Free Books,
Plus 2 Free Gifts—
just for trying the Reader Service!

⬥ HARLEQUIN® *Romance*

Get 2 Free Books,
Plus 2 Free Gifts—
just for trying the Reader Service!

Get 2 Free Books,
Plus 2 Free Gifts —
just for trying the
Reader Service!

YES! Please send me **The Hometown Hearts Collection** in Larger Print. This collection begins with 3 FREE books and 2 FREE gifts in the first shipment. Along with my 3 free books, I'll also get the next 4 books from the Hometown Hearts Collection, in LARGER PRINT, which I may either return and owe nothing, or keep for the low price of $4.99 U.S./ $5.89 CDN each plus $2.99 for shipping and handling per shipment*. If I decide to continue, about once a month for 8 months I will get 6 or 7 more books, but will only need to pay for 4. That means 2 or 3 books in every shipment will be FREE! If I decide to keep the entire collection, I'll have paid for only 32 books because 19 books are FREE! I understand that accepting the 3 free books and gifts places me under no obligation to buy anything. I can always return a shipment and cancel at any time. My free books and gifts are mine to keep no matter what I decide.

262 HCN 3432 462 HCN 3432

Name	(PLEASE PRINT)	
Address		Apt. #
City	State/Prov.	Zip/Postal Code

Signature (if under 18, a parent or guardian must sign)

Mail to the **Reader Service:**

IN U.S.A.: P.O. Box 1867, Buffalo, NY. 14240-1867
IN CANADA: P.O. Box 609, Fort Erie, Ontario L2A 5X3

* Terms and prices subject to change without notice. Prices do not include applicable taxes. Sales tax applicable in NY. Canadian residents will be charged applicable taxes. This offer is limited to one order per household. All orders subject to approval. Credit or debit balances in a customer's account(s) may be offset by any other outstanding balance owed by or to the customer. Please allow 4 to 6 weeks for delivery. Offer available while quantities last. Offer not available to Quebec residents.